Emotional Strangulation

BY

Eidahs

Cover & Editing by
Binky Ink

Binky Ink

The literary arm of Binky Productions

www.binkyproductions.com/novellas

Published in 2025 by Binky Ink
Cover and Editing by Binky Ink

ISBN: 978-1-998701-06-3

<u>WARNINGS:</u>

*This story deals with mature subject matter
such as self-harm
that some readers may find triggering.
Reader discretion is advised.*

*Other warnings include:
Strong language, blood.*

Table of Contents

CHAPTER 1

Three years earlier . . .

Jayden stepped out of the shower, wrapping his towel around his waist.

'Kai?' he called out. Jayden dried himself off and walked over to the bedroom to grab his pyjamas. 'Kai?'

On his phone, Jayden saw a message from Kai. *Had to step out for a bit. Be back soon. Love you.*

Jayden let out a small chuckle, messaging back: *Don't be gone too long.*

He settled on the couch to wait for Kai to come home. But over an hour later, Kai still wasn't back. Pacing to and fro now, Jayden fell on Kai's voicemail again.

'Kai, babe, where *are* you? We have those party favours we have to narrow down for the wedding. I can't decide these on my own and we told the planner we'd have our top three by tomorrow.'

Jayden heaved a sign as he hung up, rubbing his forehead.

His phone rang and Jayden quickly picked up without checking the caller. 'Kai?'

A female voice – far too cold and disconnected for Jayden's liking – spoke on the other end. 'Jayden Chase?'

'That's me.'

'We have on file that you are Kai Nakagawa's next of kin.'

Jayden swallowed hard. 'Next of kin? I don't understand.'

'I'm sorry, but there's been an accident.'

Jayden clamped a hand to his mouth as a sob escaped him and his vision blurred with tears. The woman continued, but all Jayden registered was the agonising, wrenching sensation in his heart that felt like he was being ripped open to bleed out.

* * *

Present Day

Jayden yawned in bed, stretching out, and for a moment, all was well. Until reality hit him again, the numbness of the past three years settling in after a heartbreaking pang. His eyes welled with tears as he glanced at his bare forearms, scarred and marred with the cuts he inflicted to quell the pain while at the same time trying to feel more than numbness.

Jayden could still hear Kai's laughter. When he closed his eyes, he could picture his face – the blue of his lover's eyes, the black hair falling flat along the sides of his beautiful face, his perfect grin when he teased Jayden.

Jayden didn't know why Kai had stepped out that night – the night the accident happened, the night Jayden lost Kai.

It was like a punch in the gut every morning. The same thing every day for the past three years. Jayden had hidden all his photos of Kai because visual reminders were still too painful and made each pang worse.

Jayden clung to the bedsheets, his arms wrapped around Kai's side of the bed, sobbing heavily as his heart was wrenched yet again this morning. He wept until his alarm went off.

With mechanical effort, Jayden got out of bed and dressed for work. His reflection in the mirror was harried. His brown hair's curls were tangled, his green eyes bloodshot, and his complexion ghostly.

He heaved a sigh and attempted to tame his unkempt hair. Perhaps the nippy air of late Fall would mitigate some of the pain, freeze his emotions so he would stop hurting so much.

Jayden kept his face impassive as he rode the bus, knowing that after work, after the routines of the day, he would come back home to an empty apartment devoid of Kai, the man who had proposed to him.

Striding into the office wearing his neutral face – screaming on the inside for someone to notice the pain he was in, yet ashamed enough to want to crawl into a corner and hide, hoping no one noticed him – Jayden began his day.

'Jayden, can I have a word?' Savannah clapped the back of Jayden's chair and walked to her office, waiting by the door.

With legs like lead, Jayden dragged himself into Savannah's office and sat down before she shut the door. She stepped up to her desk, heels clicking on the floor.

Jayden worried this was a reprimand.

'I spoke to Corporate this morning,' Savannah began, 'and they agree with me about you.'

Jayden merely nodded. If this was a reprimand, it wouldn't change the fact he would return home, eat alone, and then cry himself so tired he would fall asleep.

'You've got an efficiency no other here at the call centre does. You might not be one to take the calls, but you sort out our clients and their customers with all the dossiers like no other. Which is why . . .'

Savannah beamed at him. Jayden blinked from the surprise he felt – so this *wasn't* a reprimand.

'I want you to train the new hire.'

Great, Jayden thought with sarcasm, *human interaction.*

'He's going to be working alongside you and assisting you.'

Jayden rubbed his forehead. 'Savannah, I appreciate your trust and confidence in me, but I'm not sure I understand why I would need help. I've been the only one at that task for years.' He met his boss's gaze. 'Is this to do with last week? I told you why I was late, I had a hospital appointment to keep.'

'Jayden, this is not a reflection on you or your work.' Savannah grinned wider and she spread out her arms. 'We're expanding!'

Jayden's eyes widened. 'Oh, congratulations, then, because you are moving up the ladder, I suppose.'

Savannah nodded before frowning. 'Try to smile at our new hire, at least for today, so you don't scare him off.'

'I'll try.' Jayden looked around. 'If there's nothing else . . .'

'Actually, let me formally introduce you, he's here now.' Savannah waved a man over, walking over to the door and admitting him into her office. 'Maxwell Stratham, meet Jayden Chase, your coworker who's going to be training you.'

Jayden looked up towards the new hire.

Maxwell's obsidian eyes met Jayden's jade eyes, and the two froze. Jayden's breath caught and his heart skipped a beat. Maxwell stared as though stunned. He was absolutely gorgeous, so much it nearly made Jayden curse under his breath. The man's hair was as dark as his eyes, and his complexion a beautiful driftwood.

'Hi, uh, I'm Maxwell.' He extended his hand to Jayden, who stared at it, scared for a moment to touch the man. Then he took the hand that was offered to him and shook it, and tried to shake off the electricity that passed between them.

'Jayden.' He stood. 'I'll show you the ropes.'

Awkwardly walking around Maxwell so as to not get too close physically, Jayden marched to the small alcove that served as his corner and pulled up a second chair.

'I'll show you how it all works, and uh . . .' Jayden's gaze darted to Maxwell's lips and he had to avert his eyes. This was so wrong, he couldn't, despite needing and wanting.

'Sure.' Maxwell merely smiled at Jayden.

Jayden forced a smile on his face, feeling his cheeks strain. 'Sorry, I'm not the most . . . sociable around here.'

'No worries. We don't have to make small talk if you'd rather not, as long as you don't mind having an admirer.'

And he was interested.

Jayden wanted the admiration, but he minded too. Jayden's cheeks felt hot. He shook his head to shake himself back into focus.

'Great, then. I shall admire away, then!'

Crap, that wasn't . . . Jayden freaked out internally for a quick moment before recomposing himself. Why did Maxwell have to make him feel so . . . not numb? Jayden wanted to be numb, it was the only thing that got him through the days. He didn't want to feel . . . anything . . . for anyone.

By lunchtime, Maxwell was at his own desk and they had divvied up the tasks in two and made good progress on some of the more complex dossiers.

Jayden always took his lunch after everyone else, preferring solitude rather than having to fake pleasantries. He stood by the coffee machine, waiting for it to start pouring his coffee.

Maxwell sauntered over, all smiles. He leaned back againt the counter, observing Jayden observe the coffee machine.

'So, I have to admit, the quiet brooding demeanour intrigues me.'

Jayden let out a small laugh. 'Sorry to disappoint, but I'm boring as fuck.'

Maxwell's expression remained curious, as did his smile. 'Somehow I doubt that. And,' he leaned forward, 'I'd very much like to get to know you better, Jayden.'

Jayden worked his jaw. 'Look, it's not that I'm not interested, Maxwell – I mean, you're breathtakingly gorgeous, but . . . it's complicated.'

'I understand.' Maxwell straightened and took a step back. 'I'm sorry if I caused you any upset.'

Jayden realised his eyes were stinging.

'If ever you want to open up . . . If not, I'll respect that.'

Jayden wanted to protest, *and* confirm. 'Listen, it's not . . . it's just . . .'

Jayden went to grab his coffee, but flustered as he was, his trembling hands slipped and the mug spilled all over the floor and onto his shirt sleeve. He hissed a curse.

Maxwell grabbed some napkins to assist Jayden.

'Here.' Maxwell handed Jayden some of the napkins before grabbing more. 'Sorry . . .'

'It's fine.'

Jayden turned to grab some ice from the cafeteria fridge and placed some cubes where the hot coffee had spilled, reflexively rolling up his sleeve – and immediately regretted it upon seeing the look on Maxwell's visage. The other man's face fell and his eyes widened in worry.

Jayden pulled his sleeve back down so fast, it grazed and hurt his healing marks.

'It's nothing.'

'Nothing? Jayden, are you . . . Do you need help? Shit, that sounds so . . .' Maxwell put a fist to his mouth before starting again. 'Look, a few years back something happened and I felt guilty and would . . . hurt myself to punish myself. I get it. If ever you wanna talk or—'

'Just leave it,' snapped Jayden.

'Okay, but if ever—'

'I said leave it!' Jayden shouted, leaning forward – he saw spittle sputter from his mouth. Jaw clenched tight, he walked out of the cafeteria.

'Wait, look, I'm sorry.' Maxwell called after him.

'Tell Savannah I'm taking the rest of the day off.'

Without looking back, Jayden marched out of the office and took the bus back to his apartment, where he crumbled onto the couch, heaving sobs. A wail escaped him, the invisible fist pressing down even harder, the pain in his heart pulsing to every cell in his body.

Jayden clutched at his chest, wanting it to stop. All that he needed, all that he wanted, conflicting and warring with each other.

Unable to bear his agony any longer, Jayden rolled up his coffee-stained sleeve and stared at the marks he wanted to reopen.

* * *

Maxwell felt so guilt-ridden. He got Jayden's address from Savannah and hoped the guy wouldn't think him a stalker. Maxwell wanted to apologise.

He purchased a small bouquet of white lilies and carnations, hoping it might help, but he was so nervous as he walked up to the door.

Maxwell had been single for two years. His ex had tried to save him from himself, but it was Maxwell who needed to do the saving. In the end, it was what drew them apart.

Four lives, Maxwell had saved, but it was the one life he'd failed to save that he kept trying to save over and over throughout the years.

Maxwell lifted his hand to knock, uncertain where he would start. 'I was insistent, I came off as a jerk,' he muttered to himself. 'I understand the pain of wanting to hurt yourself.' He shook his head. 'No, too insistent again.'

Maxwell knew the fragility of one in such a state. There he'd been flirting, and all that time, Jayden had been hurting on the inside, so much he was harming himself.

It wasn't the fact that Maxwell wanted to help, wanted to save, that drew him to Jayden. The moment he'd met him, Maxwell had felt it in his entire body, a surge of emotions, magnetising him and gripping his heart. Maxwell wasn't going to let Jayden go. He just knew it in his heart, they were meant to be, *this* was meant to be.

Inexplicable as it was, it almost made Maxwell laugh, how he found he sounded like a stalker in his mind. But he knew he wanted – needed – Jayden in his life. And this small bouquet and apology was his way of letting Jayden know he wanted to respect him and be there for him.

Taking a deep breath, Maxwell knocked. And waited. He knocked again.

'Jayden?' he called out. 'Listen, I wanted to apologise. I . . . realise I must've come off as more insistent than I was trying to be. I get it, and I want to respect you. I . . . brought a peace offering.' His last statement sounded like half a question.

Maxwell sighed, muttering to himself. 'Blew it with the most gorgeous guy I've met before even getting to know him.' It squeezed his chest.

He looked around for a place to put the flowers. He noticed each apartment door had a flap for mail. That was cute, Maxwell thought. Maxwell glanced at the bouquet – it was small, it could squeeze through.

Maxwell bent and opened the mail flap . . . and froze, an invisible grip on his heart stilling it. Jayden was lying on the floor, unmoving, blood pooling on the side of his body.

Maxwell rose and kicked the door in. He burst into the apartment and darted to Jayden, skidding to a stop beside him. In Jayden's limp hand was a box knife. The young man had opened up his entire forearm.

Maxwell grabbed his phone, running to find towels, and called an ambulance. He wrapped Jayden's arm the best he could, trying to suppress the flashbacks all this was giving him.

One attempt to save four lives had caused another to die. The guilt of the accident still haunted Maxwell but he no longer punished himself for it. Even if the face of the man still haunted his dreams.

Maxwell pressed on Jayden's arm, holding it up to slow the flow of blood as he sat on the floor and waited for the ambulance to arrive. He leaned back against the couch, hoping against all odds Jayden would survive.

'Jayden, please be okay. Please don't die because of me.'

Maxwell shut his eyes and tears spilled out. The memories, the guilt, the fear and shame, the wanting to help, wanting to be forgiven. But Jayden would never be able to heal what Maxwell needed healed. Yet, perhaps Maxwell could help Jayden heal, and that would heal him.

CHAPTER 2

Jayden opened his eyes to a hospital room where he saw that his arm was completely bandaged. A pang hit him and a tremor passed through his body.

Beside the bed sat Maxwell, head bowed.

'Maxwell?'

Maxwell's head shot up and his eyes welled with tears. 'Oh, thank god. I couldn't go through witnessing another—' He stopped himself. 'I'm sorry.'

Jayden blinked. 'I don't understand.'

'I . . . . went over to your apartment to apologise. I wanted to put the flowers through the flap and . . .' He pressed his lips together.

'You found me?'

Maxwell nodded.

Jayden drew in a sharp breath. Had it not been for Jayden's abrupt tone prompting Maxwell to want to apologise to him, he might have died alone in his apartment. Tears stung his eyes.

'I didn't mean to bleed out so much,' Jayden whispered as a sob escaped him. He blurted the rest. 'I just wanted to quell the numbness. But I cut deeper than usual and I freaked as my blood pulsed out and I think I passed out at the sight of it. But I just wanted to quell the numbness.'

'I know. Hey, it's okay.' Maxwell tentatively reached out with his hand and Jayden took it. 'I've got you.'

There was a moment of quiet sobbing.

'I'm sorry,' both of them voiced. Jayden was surprised that Maxwell looked surprised.

'I shouldn't have insisted,' said Maxwell.

'You weren't at fault. I'm sorry I snapped at you.'

'You were in your rights,' said Maxwell, his voice soothing.

Jayden turned away, unable to meet Maxwell's apologetic stare. 'You say you used to . . .?'

'Yeah.'

'Like, I want to feel numb, but at the same time even that hurts because I need to feel, but feeling is agony, so I want to be numb, but then . . .' Jayden continued to stare away.

'And you want to inflict what you feel you deserve, but it's as though it's coming from outside of yourself at the same time.'

Jayden nodded. Maxwell got it. Even if his experience was not the same as Jayden's, he got it, he knew.

'How did you stop?'

'I . . . just did, I guess.'

Jayden turned back to Maxwell. 'What happened?'

Maxwell bowed his head. 'I was in the passenger seat. My friend, Daryl, lied about being under the drinking limit for driving. He would have hit a woman and her three children. I grabbed the steering wheel and swerved—' Maxwell's face contorted in chagrin. 'Right into someone else.'

Jayden inhaled sharply. He understood the guilt Maxwell felt, perhaps not entirely but at least in part.

Maxwell heaved a sob. 'They didn't even process me as a criminal. But I caused—' Maxwell shut his eyes tightly, shaking his head and speaking fast. 'I didn't want to know who he was. I didn't want to meet his family. I didn't even have the guts to show up to Daryl's hearing. But his face, the guy I crashed into, will forever be etched in my memory.'

Maxwell's pleading eyes opened. 'When I saw you lying there in your blood, I needed to save you. As though it would make up for what I had caused.'

Jayden reflexively reached a hand up to Maxwell's face. 'You saved a family. But I understand survivor's guilt.'

Maxwell wiped his eyes and met Jayden's. 'What happened, Jayden? To cause you such hurt?'

Jayden stared at his bandaged arm. 'Someone ran over my fiancé.'

Maxwell drew in a sharp breath. 'Jayden,' he whispered.

'I was in the shower when it happened. Kai left me a note that he was stepping out for a bit. When I got the call about the accident, it felt like everything was shattering.'

'Oh, Jayden.'

'The driver's in prison, so . . . and well, I . . . well, numb.' Jayden lifted his arm and a jolt of pain shot through it. He cried out.

'Jayden, you need a nurse?' Maxwell was on his feet.

'No, it's fine. Just pain.'

Maxwell hesitated. 'Listen, I'll let you rest.'

'You can stay.' Jayden hoped Maxwell understood what he was trying to say.

Maxwell sat back down. His earnest eyes were so captivating, Jayden, for a moment, forgot the physical and emotional pain he was in.

'The first thing that helped me stop hurting myself,' Maxwell began slowly after a few moments had passed, 'was to express what I was needing and feeling directly.'

He *had* understood.

And a dam opened up in Jayden's heart.

'I'm scared to be left alone because it hurts so much inside, this emotional pain, and I'm scared of doing worse to myself without wanting to. Had you not found me . . .' Jayden began weeping openly again. 'I need you here with me, you're the only one who gets it, and . . . I feel safe around you. I can't explain it, but you make me feel safe.'

Maxwell blinked, then offered Jayden a wan smile. 'When you open up, you open up.'

Jayden let out a laugh before sobering. 'Maxwell, I'm going to be honest with you. I have not let myself feel much of anything for three years.'

'Three,' Maxwell repeated. 'About the time I started . . . you know . . . too.'

Jayden nodded. 'Some divine timing, huh? I . . . I have not felt like I was living all this time. And then I met you and . . . I am just drawn to you and . . . I started feeling things again. I don't want to feel because it hurts too much.'

Maxwell wrapped his arms around Jayden – the gesture was so comforting, Jayden let himself relax in the man's arms.

'I get it,' Maxwell soothed. 'You know what, though? It is when you start to feel again that it heals. I know it hurts.' He pulled away. 'Though I can't imagine how I might feel if I lost the man I loved. Just know that I'm here, in whatever capacity you need me.'

'Under normal circumstances, I'd ask you out, and flirt back. Right now . . .' Jayden's vision blurred. 'Hold me, keep me safe, comfort me?'

'Okay,' whispered Maxwell.

* * *

Maxwell helped Jayden get home a few days later, and Jayden asked him if he was comfortable assisting him, since one arm was out of commission until the stitches would be out. To Jayden's relief, Maxwell agreed to help.

Jayden didn't know how he would have coped alone. It was more for the emotional support than anything else. Jayden kept imagining himself hurting himself, the intrusive thoughts invading his mind with him doing even worse to himself – not because he wanted to, just because he felt horrified and his fear fed on that.

Maxwell would pass by in the morning before work and then in the evening to prepare a meal. They ate together, lounged around together. Sometimes, Maxwell slept over on the couch.

At Jayden's behest, Maxwell told folks at work that Jayden had been robbed and attacked. In Jayden's mind, it was the truth. He had been robbed of his fiancé three years prior and he had attacked himself.

Jayden put the bowl he'd been eating from down onto the coffee table and leaned back. 'That salad was delicious.'

Sitting beside Jayden on the couch, Maxwell smiled. 'I'm glad you enjoyed it.' He looked around. 'Let me get some cleaning done for you.'

Jayden stopped him with a hand on his knee. 'No, I just want you near me.'

'Okay.'

Jayden leaned into Maxwell who wrapped his arms around him. They had become cuddle buddies in the past couple of weeks, and had grown a lot closer emotionally. Both were still guarded with some walls up, but they were more liberal with their affection towards each other. It almost reminded Jayden of Kai, of how fast they had grown attached to each other.

Jayden would be stuck with the stitches for a whole other week – three weeks total – and then he still had to be careful for a week just to be sure. He had sliced down a lot and they had put in internal sutures too.

Jayden had never hurt himself that deeply before. The guilt of wanting to be held and touched by another man – and the secret Jayden kept from this other man – made him feel like he should have died the night Maxwell found him.

Jayden scratched his head and flakes drizzled from his scalp.

'Have you been able to wash your hair?' asked Maxwell.

'Is it that obvious that I've gone two weeks without washing it?' Jayden grinned as a chuckle escaped him. 'I mean, I have to cover up my arm with a plastic bag, so . . . I've let water fall on my hair, but . . .' He scratched again.

'Okay. Jayden?' Maxwell pushed him gently off him and stood, offering his hand. 'It's time to wash your hair. And I'm going to scrub it like it's never been scrubbed before.'

That garnered a laugh from Jayden. Maxwell's smile was infectious, and Jayden beamed the whole time Maxwell helped him.

Jayden changed into his bathing suit to be comfortable and decent. Maxwell held the shower head over Jayden's head with one hand, and with the other, passed his fingers through Jayden's curly hair, massaging his scalp. The sensation was calming, soothing.

When Maxwell was done, he helped lather Jayden's body and rinsed with the shower head. All the while both being careful of the arm, which had a plastic bag wrapped around, it to keep it up and dry.

Jayden stepped out of the shower, feeling refreshed. Maxwell took a towel and wrapped it around Jayden's shoulders.

'All better?'

'Definitely. Thanks.'

The two beamed at each other, getting lost in their gazes, before sobering. Jayden's heart was pumping so fast. He stood dripping wet, almost naked before Maxwell, whose eyes travelled the length of Jayden's body, lingering on his crotch before averting his gaze.

Jayden leaned forward, his lips grazing Maxwell's. Maxwell inhaled and exhaled quickly, his gaze smouldering – it made Jayden's body react with want. Jayden's entire body was alight with a fire only Kai had known how to ignite before now.

The two kept teasing their lips, nearly touching, a hair's breadth away, pulling back and leaning forward again.

Maxwell closed his eyes, whispering, 'Jayden. If I kiss you now, I don't know that I'll be able to stop.'

He turned his head away and took a step back.

Jayden realised his arm was throbbing. Pumping his blood with thoughts or actions of whatever might happen between him and Maxwell was probably best to be avoided until he was told his wound had healed.

'You're right, it's not a good idea.' Jayden lifted his arm. He could hear the disappointment in his own voice.

Maxwell tilted Jayden's chin up with soft fingers. 'It's not for lack of wanting.'

That tightened the sensation in Jayden's chest as much as it made his heart soar.

Maxwell leaned in and kissed Jayden's forehead. The gesture was comforting, but it wasn't enough.

Maxwell left the bathroom, leaving Jayden to dress alone. Jayden placed one hand on the steamy tiles, taking a deep breath. Resisting Maxwell had become near impossible, so much so that now it was Maxwell who was resisting Jayden.

* * *

The day the stitches came out, the nurse confirmed Jayden's wound was healed, but advised him to be careful for the next week or so, given the circumstances. Jayden was to be on sick leave for another month, with a therapist visit scheduled every week. They required Jayden to keep a log of his state of mind for their evaluations. And as per, since Maxwell had been helping him, they had asked that he continue to keep an eye on Jayden.

'I mean, part of me is relieved you get to continue to check up on me,' Jayden said as they walked to Maxwell's car.

'It's not like I would stop caring for you, Jayden.' Maxwell's smile was warm. He opened the door for Jayden before walking over to the driver's side. Jayden clocked the way Maxwell had phrased it, and it made his stomach whoop . . . and also flipped it upside down.

He leaned back against the headrest. 'Part of me is embarrassed that I can't be trusted on my own.'

Maxwell placed a hand on Jayden's thigh. 'You *can* be trusted on your own, Jayden, but they are concerned because you purposely . . . I understand the shame one feels from hurting themselves. You're safe with me.'

Jayden had to stop himself from lunging for Maxwell's lips. He still jerked forward, and to disguise the abrupt movement, he placed his hand on Maxwell's face and pecked his cheek quickly, before retreating into his seat and swallowing down the urges.

Jayden glanced over at Maxwell and his heart palpitated when he realised Maxwell was gripping the steering wheel hard, his features as intense as when they had shared their near bathroom kiss a week earlier.

Maxwell let out a slow breath before starting the car.

Chapter 3

As autumn turned to winter, Maxwell continued to come by to help Jayden, not just because he had been tasked to, but because he cared for him. His feelings were growing by the day, developing into something deeper.

Jayden sometimes called Maxwell at work to verify some dossiers were being well managed by him.

'You checking up on *me* now?' Maxwell had chuckled over the phone.

Maxwell spent most of his days at Jayden's apartment – Jayden had even given him his spare keys – and he couldn't deny the attraction or developing feelings any longer.

Maxwell was uncertain if he should make a move on Jayden when he was still so vulnerable – it wouldn't be fair to either of them. Jayden had been given another month off work, and he seemed to enjoy the time of relaxation it entailed – or perhaps, Maxwell hoped, he enjoyed having Maxwell look after him.

It was as though they were dating, except without the benefits of dating and without the responsibilities of dating. But Maxwell wanted both.

The two were standing in Jayden's small kitchen. Maxwell was leaning against the counter.

'It's been nearly three months,' said Maxwell. 'You still not up for returning to work?'

Jayden pressed his lips together. 'I'm not ready to say that I'm okay because then it means I'll be alone again.'

'You won't be alone,' Maxwell comforted, understanding the loneliness he himself felt when he thought of not checking in on Jayden every day anymore. 'I'm here for you, always.'

Jayden's eyes brimmed with tears. 'I don't deserve you,' he whispered.

Maxwell tilted his head, cupping Jayden's face. 'Why would you think that? You do deserve me.'

Jayden shook his head. 'I still love Kai.'

A pang hit Maxwell harder than he anticipated. 'I understand,' he said softly as his eyes stung hot. He blinked, turning away.

'But I need to be touched, I need to be held, I need . . .' Jayden stepped forward, bringing his lips close to Maxwell's.

'Jayden,' Maxwell whispered, tilting his head forward, yet still resisting. He wanted to hear him say that he needed *him*.

A sob escaped Jayden. 'I'm desperate, Maxwell.'

Jayden pressed a hard kiss to Maxwell's lips and it took Maxwell's breath away. Jayden wrapped his arms around the other man, as his tongue slid into Maxwell's mouth to twin with his, but Maxwell steeled himself and pulled back quickly.

'Jayden, I won't take advantage of you when you're feeling desperate. It won't be fair to either of us.'

Breathing heavily, Maxwell leaned the side of his head on Jayden's temple, holding him tightly. Both breathed in elatedly, feeling each other out. Jayden rubbed himself on Maxwell, weeping and spasming, and Maxwell let out a moan.

'Fuck, Jayden,' he whispered. His grip on him tightened further, but Maxwell held strong, never moving and never relenting to his desire. 'I am so sorry, it just feels wrong to do this when you are in this state.'

Jayden pulled away from the embrace abruptly and walked over to grab a glass. He poured himself some water and downed it in one go.

Maxwell put a hand to his mouth – his lips still tingled with the lingering sensation of Jayden's lips on them. He looked away as Jayden walked over to the couch and plopped down.

Jayden stared down at his arm, lifting the sleeve and passing his hand along his long scar. Maxwell's heart quickened. He didn't want to be the cause of Jayden feeling the need to hurt himself, and he immediately regretted turning him down.

When Maxwell had been in such a state, anything could send him spiralling into emotions that felt like they were strangulating him. And if he felt strangled by emotions, he felt an urge to hurt himself. Maxwell didn't want to be a cause of emotional strangulation to Jayden, he wanted to be that lungful of air that made him feel like he could breathe again.

Jayden pulled his sleeve back down and looked over at Maxwell. 'Hold me?'

'That, I can do.'

Maxwell joined Jayden on the couch. It took all his self-control to merely wrap his arms around him. He wanted him so badly, it was beginning to be agonising.

After some deep and quickened breaths where it was evident both were resisting each other, the two fell asleep on the couch.

* * *

Maxwell had a hard time focusing at work the next day. He rubbed his temples, sighing.

Savannah sauntered over. 'Hey, if it's starting to be too much, take some time off.' She had a pointed stare that conveyed at once her concern as it did her need as a manager for her employees to be at their best.

After several more hours of failing at working, Maxwell clocked out early. He was putting on his jacket when Cindy from the finance department walked over.

'I've forwarded everything about that new client to help keep things organised,' she announced.

'Thank you, Cindy. I'll have a look at it in the morning.' Maxwell fixed the collar of his jacket. Cindy eyed Maxwell warily. 'Do I have something on my face?' he asked carefully.

'It's just, it mustn't be easy. You've been spending a lot of time with Jayden, I hear.' Cindy shook her head. 'He hasn't been able to move on. I can't imagine if you got close . . .'

Maxwell narrowed his eyes. 'What happens or doesn't happen between me and Jayden is between me and Jayden.'

'I get that. Sorry to pry. Just . . . be careful. He's vulnerable.'

'I haven't been taking advantage of him, if that's your concern,' Maxwell said through gritted teeth. He didn't like the implications.

'That's not it. Look, be careful for *you*. You don't deserve to be messed around either. Jayden is as much on life support as Kai is right now . . .'

The rest was lost as the air left Maxwell's lungs. A pressure squeezed his chest so hard, he put a hand to his heart.

Maxwell was too distraught to drive; he left his car at the office and took the bus to Jayden's. He strode in, breathing hard, having run from the bus stop.

Jayden looked up at him, surprised. He stood, brows furrowing in concern as he came face to face with Maxwell.

'Why didn't you tell me he was alive?!' Maxwell demanded, his voice raised.

Jayden swallowed hard, his throat bobbing.

Maxwell pointed behind him. 'I just learnt today that Kai is on life support! Why did you never tell me? This changes everything!'

'How does it change anything between us?' pleaded Jayden.

'It changes that instead of grieving the death of the man you loved, your fiancé is still alive.'

'Maxwell,' Jayden bowed his head. 'I'm sorry I never told you.'

'Why?' Maxwell's tone came out more plea than demand, and his eyes stung with tears.

'He's in a coma,' Jayden said softly. 'His family is keeping him on life support. If he ever wakes – and after three years that's a big if – chances are he's going to be a vegetable.'

Jayden took a step forward, taking Maxwell's hand. 'What am I supposed to do? I don't even know why he had to step out that night. I've put my life on hold, unable to move on, *unwilling* to move on, until I met you.'

'No!' Maxwell took a step back, pushing Jayden's hand away so hard he might as well have slapped it away. 'This makes me the other man. I can't be that.'

Jayden's brows creased. 'You don't want me?'

'Want you?!' Maxwell threw his hands up and grabbed his hair, shaking his head in disbelief. 'Jayden, I'm falling for you.'

Jayden drew in a sharp breath.

'You still love Kai, a man who is *alive*. I cannot and will not make you choose.' Maxwell couldn't do that.

Feeling like his heart was being squeezed by a vice, Maxwell turned and left the apartment. Jayden called after him.

* * *

Jayden hurried after Maxwell who was walking so fast down the sidewalk he could have been jogging.

'Maxwell, wait, please!'

Maxwell spun around. 'We can't keep this as it is – this, us,' he motioned between them, 'whatever this is between us, Jayden. But I hate ultimatums. I can't make you choose, I can't do that to you. You're already hurting enough as it is. But I'm hurting too.' He placed a hand on his chest.

The flash of high beams and the screech of tires stilled Jayden's heart as a car slammed into Maxwell from behind. Maxwell's body bent backwards, and he hit his head on the windshield before rolling over and falling onto the street.

Jayden's scream was desperate as he ran over to Maxwell, cradling his head in his arms.

'Maxwell, please, stay with me, in all the ways.'

That moment hit Jayden harder than that car hit Maxwell, and he knew what he felt for him.

'Jayden,' Maxwell whispered.

Tears pouring down Jayden's face, he cried, 'Maxwell, I'm falling for you too, okay? Please stay with me. Maxwell!'

Maxwell's eyes fluttered closed and his body went limp.

The rest was a blur.

An ambulance arrived. It was confirmed that the driver skidded on black ice. He didn't run after hitting. The man kept apologising, Jayden could hear him, and he gave himself in to the police.

Jayden rode in the ambulance with Maxwell, holding his hand, muttering softly to him.

'Maxwell, please stay with me. I love both you and Kai. I can't lose another man I love to a car accident. Please be okay. Just please live.'

Jayden wept as Maxwell was taken by the medics, his heart wrenching. He brought his hands to his face. At that moment, he wanted to open up his arm again, he wanted to watch himself bleed out, because he *felt* like he was bleeding out *right now*. The emotional turmoil he was in was agonisingly more than any physical wound he had ever inflicted upon himself.

When the doctor said Jayden could see Maxwell, he nearly tripped, scurrying to the room.

Maxwell was conscious. Jayden sobbed out in relief. He hurried over to his side and took his hand.

'Maxwell.' Jayden cupped his face. 'Thank god you're alive.'

Maxwell smiled wanly. 'Doc says it's a mild concussion and I might experience . . .' He made air quotes, 'Head related issues.' He chuckled mirthlessly. 'Not even close to what I deserve, a fitting punishment though to be hit like—'

'Stop it!' Jayden brought Maxwell's hand to his mouth and brushed a gentle kiss on it. 'Who's self-loathing now?'

Maxwell reached for Jayden's face. 'I love you. But I won't make you choose.'

'I love you both,' admitted Jayden. Even if told to choose, Jayden could not.

Maxwell turned his face away, pained. 'I don't want to be the other man.'

'You already are. We're already involved.'

Jayden again felt like saying 'Please stay with me,' but refrained from begging.

Maxwell pulled Jayden to him suddenly and engulfed his mouth in a searing kiss. Jayden let out a moan as their tongues twined, and he closed his eyes, feeling a wash of relief. Maxwell pulled away abruptly, face scrunched as tears poured from his eyes.

'That was a goodbye kiss, Jayden.'

And again, Jayden felt like he was losing everything, losing himself.

'Let's not make any rash decisions, just for today.'

Maxwell's jaw was set tight. He closed his eyes. 'I don't want to lose you,' he whispered, 'but I have to let you go.'

'Then I'll go,' said Jayden. 'But I'll be back. That's a promise.'

Before Maxwell could voice any counter-arguments, Jayden grabbed his coat and left.

He leaned against the hospital wall, his breath syncopated. Maxwell continuously saying he would not force a choice on Jayden . . . only made him love him more.

<u>CHAPTER 4</u>

Jayden visited Maxwell again and neither mentioned the kiss nor the possibility of parting ways. They avoided any talk of their non-relationship or their love for each other.

Finally, it was the day Maxwell was being sent home.

Jayden offered him his hand. 'Let's go for a walk before we go. There is someone I want you to meet.'

'Kai?'

'Yes, Kai.'

Maxwell nodded mechanically. He was uncertain how he felt about meeting the man with whose fiancé he had fallen in love. Jayden for his part had removed all reminders of Kai from his apartment, and Maxwell had not pushed him to show him either – he wanted to respect Jayden's space. Maxwell wondered if he and Kai were similar in any way.

Maxwell followed Jayden to the room where Kai was plugged to life support.

As soon as Maxwell's eyes landed on Kai's face, his world came crashing down like the screech of tires and the shatter of glass.

Maxwell put a hand to his mouth as he flashed back to that night.

* * *

'You're going awfully fast, man. Are you sure you only had one beer?'

'Nope!' Daryl burped. He leaned forward, pressing on the gas even more. Everything outside was speeding by and Maxwell's stomach lurched.

'Oh my god, Daryl! Okay, pull over. I'm driving.'

'Nah, man, it's cool. You think I can make that yellow?'

'You're going to get us killed!' Maxwell shouted. 'Press on the breaks now!'

Daryl only sped faster. The traffic lights turned red. Daryl never slowed.

Maxwell saw the woman and her children before Daryl did. And Daryl froze, the car speeding right towards them.

Maxwell grabbed the steering wheel, praying they would all survive this, and spun the car around so fast, it hitched up onto the sidewalk and barrelled right into a young man, whose eyes widened in shock before he was crammed between a wall and the car.

The car lifted off the ground, and as the man's head came down on the windshield, the glass shattered. Maxwell covered his face to protect it from the glass, but the man's face would forever be embedded in his mind.

* * *

Maxwell was trembling. He backed away to the wall as his eyes blurred with tears.

'I know it's a shock,' said Jayden.

'You have no idea,' whispered Maxwell.

'But I wanted you to see him, the man who is the reason I keep . . . why I've been . . .' Jayden sighed.

Jayden had no clue. How was Maxwell going to tell him?

Jayden sat down beside Kai and took his hand. Kai was half-Japanese. Jayden had described him as having blue eyes and black hair, and a mixed Asian look. Maxwell never imagined that Japanese man, whose medium-length hair now fell flat on a white hospital pillow, would be the same man whose face would forever be imprinted in Maxwell's mind.

Jayden brought Kai's hand to his heart. 'Kai, I . . . I tried, Kai – tried to be brave, tried to be strong. But I hurt myself again. And then I . . . I've fallen for someone. I love you so much, I always will, but when a car crashed into him too, I realised in that moment of impact, that I loved him. I am so sorry, Kai.'

Jayden bowed his head, tears pouring from his eyes.

'I can't do this anymore, this living yet non-living. I need you to either wake up or . . . move on – because *I* need to move on. I love you and I need you, but I also love another man. I need to love and be forgiven.'

'I'm the one who needs to be forgiven,' whispered Maxwell, gritting his teeth.

He bolted out of the room, unable to remain any longer. Jayden went after him and tugged on his arm, turning him around.

Maxwell gaped at Jayden, his breath shaking.

'Maxwell, please. I love you both and want you both in my life. I know it's . . . I didn't want to hide this from you anymore.'

'You don't know who Kai is to me, do you?'

Jayden furrowed his brows in confusion. He shook his head.

'Fate is cruel and twisted. I think it's best we parted ways, Jayden,' Maxwell pointed towards the room, 'because *I'm* the reason Kai is in that state.'

Jayden gasped sharply, realising what Maxwell meant.

'I have caused you both so much heartache. I don't deserve you. I'm the reason you've been . . . hurting yourself.'

'But you saved me!' insisted Jayden. The one life Maxwell thought he'd failed, the one he kept trying to save through others, had been alive all this time. Kai's face that night tugged at him and broke his heart anew, because comatose as Kai was, he wasn't saved.

'You wouldn't have needed me to save you had I not rammed that car into your fiancé!' Maxwell shouted. He put a hand to his mouth, tears pouring down his face. 'I'm sorry, Jayden – for ever entering your lives. I'm so sorry I caused all this. It's all my fault. I'm so sorry.'

'Maxwell, stop it.' Jayden held firm on his hand. 'You saved a family. You weren't to know your friend was too drunk. You weren't to know Kai was there.'

'You'll come to hate me.'

Jayden shook his head. 'This doesn't change how I feel about you. I want you in my life.'

'Give it a few hours, a few days, and then see if you still feel the same way. I won't blame you for resenting me, for blaming me.'

'As far as I'm concerned, your friend caused this, not you.'

'*I* swerved the car around and onto Kai,' Maxwell seethed in Jayden's face. He sputtered out, livid, '*I am the reason he is in a coma. I am the reason that your life is on hold and Kai is on life support. I* am the reason you cut yourself and make yourself bleed. *I* am the reason Kai might never wake up, or worse, be brain-dead when he does.'

Maxwell hated himself right now and wanted Jayden to hate him just as much.

'I know what you're doing, Maxwell, because like you told me, we are alike in that way. But this doesn't change how I feel.'

'No. I can't do this. We need to take a step back from each other. You and Kai don't deserve for me to be in your lives – you deserve better. I deserve for you to be out of my life.' He passed a hand through his hair. 'I don't know what's crueler, loving a man whose comatose fiancé is the man I hit or—'

'When that car hit you, I knew I loved you!' shouted Jayden.

'I don't deserve your love!' Maxwell shouted back, his self-loathing making his hands tremble.

Maxwell marched away from Jayden and out of the hospital, wanting to disappear from the face of the earth. Jayden called after him but gave no pursuit. Good, Maxwell needed Jayden to hate him, and then they could both move on.

* * *

Work was slow and Maxwell's heart kept sinking. Jayden had sent him a text message, stating, *You're right. We should spend some time apart.*

An email came in, addressed to the entire staff – from Jayden. It was one of resignation, where Jayden was saying goodbye to everyone.

Maxwell's heart rose to his throat. The vehement anger he had spewed at Jayden – what if it had driven Jayden to the edge? Maxwell hated himself more than before.

He bolted out of the office and went straight to Jayden's apartment. He looked up at Jayden's window from outside to see if he saw movement inside.

'Jayden? Jayden!' Maxwell called out.

He ran into the apartment building, fumbling with his keys. He dropped them as he tried to get them in. He called Jayden's name again but there was no response. He shoved the door open just as it clicked unlocked and barged in, terrified he would find Jayden lying in a pool of his blood again.

'Maxwell?'

Jayden emerged from the small office with a woman who held a clipboard. The woman seemed to be assessing Maxwell, while Jayden looked stunned.

Maxwell let out a shaking breath and leaned against the wall for support. His shaking legs felt like they would give way under him at any moment. 'Oh thank god.'

'I will speak with you next week,' the woman told Jayden. 'Remember, it's up to you to pursue or not . . .' she cast a quick glance Maxwell's way. 'But I am glad to see you take out your photos. Don't hide your past – face it, so you can gain clarity on your future.'

She offered Maxwell a mild smile and left, closing the door softly.

Maxwell slid down the wall to a crouch, shedding a few tears.

'Maxwell, what's going on? Are you okay?'

Maxwell stood quickly, marching to Jayden, his face so close. 'I thought . . . with the message and the email . . . I was scared that you might—' Maxwell pressed his lips together, trying to control his heaving. He whispered in a half sob, 'I thought you were going to kill yourself.'

Jayden inhaled sharply. 'No. I thought a few days apart might do us good, but I was going to call you so we could discuss what we both discovered at the hospital.'

Maxwell whimpered. 'You don't hate me? *Still* don't hate me?'

'Maxwell, I love you,' asserted Jayden, taking Maxwell's face in his hands.

'Jayden, I love you.' Maxwell was agonised by reality. He leaned forward, his breath hitching. 'You have no idea how much I want you right now.'

'You have no idea how much I want you,' declared Jayden.

'But I caused—'

'No, you didn't – your friend did. And knowing it, it's a shock, but I still fell in love with you while still loving my comatose fiancé.'

Jayden's eyes showed pleading, desperation, and the need that Maxwell felt himself. Their faces, their lips, were so close. Maxwell's breath syncopated.

Jayden lowered his voice, as though he were issuing a threat. 'And just so you know, no matter how hard you try to make me hate you, I can't.'

Maxwell leaned his forehead on Jayden's. 'I have been resisting you for so long. How fate brought us together, it hurts, it's cruel. How can you stand here and feel the way you do about me when I . . .' Maxwell stared at Jayden, both of them gasping.

Then they both lunged for each other and Maxwell claimed Jayden's lips, pressing his hands on his face. Both groaned as, this time, neither stopped nor resisted. Maxwell was done stopping himself. He wanted Jayden.

Tears mingled with their tongues as their naked limbs tangled in the sheets. Maxwell was amazed by how affectionate and sensual Jayden was towards him, and his heart broke as pang after pang of feeling undeserving hit him.

The moment was beautiful, and it lasted a long time. As both came down from their euphoria, they straddled each other, holding each other tightly, and weeping.

Jayden pulled away to wipe Maxwell's tears with his thumb. 'I want you in my life,' he whispered. 'I know it's complicated, but I need you.'

'I need you too, Jayden.' Maxwell kissed him fervently.

They continued to hold each other and eventually lay down and fell asleep. Their nap was interrupted by Jayden's cell phone.

* * *

Jayden reached for his phone, all while keeping an arm draped over Maxwell's chest.

'Hello?'

He looked over at Maxwell and nibbled his pec. He smiled cheekily, biting his lower lip as the woman on the phone introduced herself.

Her next words paralysed Jayden, and he was uncertain whether he was grieved or relieved by her news.

'Okay, thanks. I'll be right over.'

Jayden hung up, staring down at his phone.

'Everything okay?' Maxwell brushed some hair from Jayden's face. 'Jayden?'

Jayden looked up at Maxwell, eyes already filled with tears caused by this unknown emotion. 'It was the hospital . . . Kai . . .' His voice caught in his throat.

Maxwell gently brushed the backs of his fingers on Jayden's face, his eyes conveying empathy.

'Kai is awake.'

Maxwell gaped back, stopping his hand. Jayden could guess some of the thoughts racing through Maxwell's mind because Jayden's was whirling.

Jayden dashed out of bed and dressed as quickly as he could without another word. When he left, Maxwell was lying on his back, staring up at the ceiling, but even while Jayden's heart clenched from the sight, he needed to go see Kai.

CHAPTER 5

Jayden hesitated at the hospital room's door. What was he going to say, how would he begin? His hands were trembling. He pulled on his sweater's sleeve, holding it tightly in his fist.

Coat draped over one arm, Jayden took a deep breath and walked into the room.

Kai, bleary-eyed, looked up at Jayden. The nurse hadn't told Jayden what to expect, only that Kai was conscious and coherent, and that Jayden could visit him anytime.

'Hey,' Jayden said softly.

'Hey,' Kai replied just as softly.

Jayden hesitated before continuing.

'I'm told three years have passed.' Kai smiled sheepishly, his blue eyes so bright and full of hope. 'You'll have to catch me up on all the latest celebrity gossip.'

A sob escaped Jayden and he put a hand to his mouth.

Kai furrowed his brows, the look he had when he was barely containing his emotions. He whispered, 'Jayden, baby.'

Jayden ran over to Kai and flung his arms around him, heaving uncontrollably. Kai wrapped his arms around Jayden, stroking his back. The clench in Jayden's chest tightened and squeezed harder than ever before, while at the same time releasing a dam of pent-up and suppressed sorrow.

Jayden lifted his face, wiping his eyes. 'Sorry. I'm just such a mess, you have no idea.'

'It's okay,' Kai soothed, brushing his knuckles on Jayden's tear-streaked cheek.

Kai took a beat. 'They had me do a bunch of tests as soon as they saw I was awake. Asked so many questions, checked so many things. I still have more examinations to undergo, though. They wanted to evaluate my state of mind. I've been deemed miraculously of sound mind.'

Kai chuckled. Jayden could only nod and listen as Kai continued.

'I felt groggy, like I was hung over. But after three years, I have healed, except, well, my muscles are a bit of a mush on my lower body. The fractures in my legs and crushed ribs healed a long time ago. Still, I'm going to need physio for my legs.'

'But you have feeling in them?'

'Yeah. Except my muscles are slow to respond. My upper body's fine, as you can see.' He waved his arms about for a few seconds before wrapping them around Jayden again. 'I started moving again mid-interview. My lower body has yet to respond properly. It's . . . snailed.' Kai frowned. 'At least I'm alive. And I've got you by my side, Jayden.'

'That's amazing,' Jayden awed. 'That you're alive, awake, and . . .' He cleared his throat. 'So you remember who you are, and me, obviously.'

'And the accident.'

Jayden pulled back, uncertain what Kai would think if he knew Jayden had just made love to the man who put him in a coma for three years.

Kai's eyes grew distant. 'I saw the car swerve away from a family and . . . The last thing I remember was that guy's face. He wasn't the driver, and the doc confirmed he was the passenger.' Kai furrowed his brows. 'He looked so horrified, terrified, exactly what I felt in that moment before the air was sucked out of me, and then . . . nothing.' His voice went from solemn to hopeful. 'Here we are now, three years later, eh? Wow, three years have gone by.'

Kai lifted Jayden's chin gently. 'Do I . . . still have a fiancé?'

Jayden froze. And then realised he had taken too long to answer.

Kai downcast his eyes. 'I see.'

'Kai, it's complicated. I . . . never stopped loving you. I put my life *on hold* for you, but I . . . started seeing someone from work. Someone new, new hire. And . . . I resisted for a long time.'

'How long?' asked Kai, his tone disconcertingly calm.

'A few months. We've been . . . resisting the attraction, but we . . . got together . . . more recently.'

'Do you love him?'

Jayden pressed his lips together. He wept out, 'I love you both.'

There was a moment where neither of them spoke. Jayden wondered if he'd been too forthcoming, or if his decision to come clean now was best. He couldn't imagine hiding Maxwell from Kai, it just didn't feel right to lie about him.

'Does he know about me?' Kai asked at length.

'He does.' An invisible knife twisted in Jayden's heart. 'It's . . . complicated.' Jayden met his fiancé's gaze. 'I had sex with him.'

Kai nodded carefully. It was unnerving how calm he was staying.

Finally, Kai spoke softly. 'I don't blame you. Had I not gone . . . for a walk, that car would have hit no one. That accident was of my own doing.'

'Don't say that. You couldn't have predicted getting hit by a car when out for some fresh air.'

'Yeah, I certainly didn't predict that.' Kai's eyes grew unfocused. Then he scrunched his face as tears welled in his eyes, and he bowed his head, sobbing.

Jayden and Kai wrapped their arms around each other again, weeping for a long time.

Kai pressed his cheek to Jayden's, breathing in deeply as he continued to weep. He kissed Jayden's cheek, then moved to align their lips, and pressed for a tender kiss.

Jayden reciprocated with a soft kiss. Kai kissed Jayden again, and Jayden kissed quickly back. This back-and-forth of tentative kisses continued for several minutes, every time clenching and releasing the invisible vice around Jayden's heart. And then they were devouring each other heatedly.

Jayden sobbed into Kai's mouth as Kai moaned, his hand gliding up Jayden's arm. Kai stopped when his thumb touched the raised line that was Jayden's scar.

Kai pulled back as Jayden retracted his hand, but Kai caught it and pushed the sleeve up. His eyes widened.

'What happened? Jayden, this looks recent.'

Jayden hesitated, considering telling the lie he had Maxwell tell at work.

'Jayden? Please tell me what happened.'

'I did this to myself,' Jayden admitted, his voice barely above a whisper.

Kai put a hand to his mouth as more tears welled in his eyes.

Jayden continued. 'I would do it when I wanted to feel more than numb but also wanted to forget the emotional pain I was in. It was a way to punish myself.'

Kai exhaled shakily through his nose, shutting his eyes tight.

'The night I did this . . . I didn't mean to cut that deep. I did it because I met Maxwell and I was so hungry for affection and felt such a need, and I felt so guilty . . . and then he came and found me. Else I would have bled out.'

Kai let out a sob. 'Then I have *him* to thank for keeping my fiancé alive.' Kai's expression changed. 'Is he . . . the other man in your life?'

Jayden nodded. 'Kai, I'm so sorry.' Jayden realised he had dumped all this hurtful info on Kai. The squeeze in his chest gripped him so hard, he let out a pained wail.

Kai wrapped his arms around Jayden. 'I don't blame you,' was all he said before the two fell into silent weeping.

* * *

It had been several days since Kai had awoken. Maxwell had left Jayden's apartment shortly after Jayden had left him alone in bed. Maxwell had sent him several messages, but Maxwell didn't know if Jayden was purposely ignoring him or just too busy to call him.

Maxwell felt fear, and guilt – it was pang after pang of emotions, and he didn't know what to do anymore. They hadn't spoken about taking a step back from each other since their moment of sexual intimacy. Maxwell wondered if Jayden was doing just that, taking a step back from Maxwell now that Kai had awoken.

A knock came at the door. Maxwell was surprised to see Jayden. There was relief mixed into that, and fear.

'Can we talk?'

'Come in.' Maxwell admitted Jayden and the two settled on the sofa in the living room. 'I was beginning to wonder if you were ignoring me.'

'No, I . . . I told Kai about us.'

Maxwell took that in. '*Is* there an us?'

'I'd like there to be,' said Jayden. 'I want to keep seeing you.'

'You've broken things off with Kai, then?' Maxwell asked, deducing.

'Actually,' began Jayden. Maxwell's heart sank. 'Kai and I want to start fresh.'

Maxwell let out a slow exhale. 'Does Kai know you want to keep seeing me?'

'He knows how I feel about you.'

Maxwell stood abruptly and backed away. 'I will not be the other man, Jayden. You intend to cheat on your fiancé with me? With *me*? Does he know who I am, what I did to him?'

'No.'

'I'm not sneaking around behind Kai's back, Jayden. I thought maybe you chose me of your own volition – because I won't force this choice on you – but you are choosing *him*, and then you want *me* on the side? That's not fair to either of us.'

'I could tell him—'

'Whether you tell him or not, you want us both, and I don't know how I feel about that.'

Jayden stood and took hold of Maxwell's hand as he cried out, 'But I love you!'

'I love you too!' declared Maxwell.

'Then please consider this.' Jayden leaned his forehead on Maxwell's.

'I don't want to be your little bit on the side. If we do this, Jayden, Kai has to know that you're seeing us both.'

'You know, for someone who doesn't want to force a decision on me, you sure seem to push towards having me choose Kai over you, the way you've been talking. Maxwell, I love you both and want you both in my life. That's all I know, okay?'

Jayden's lips grazed Maxwell's. Maxwell inhaled sharply, already elated. Just that small tingle felt so good, especially now that they had shared sexual intimacy and made love. Maxwell had longed for Jayden all these days. And he found that he had no self-restraint left to resist him.

Their lips met in a fiery exchange that would lead to more lovemaking if Maxwell didn't put a stop to it – and he *couldn't* put a stop to it, he didn't want to.

Hands travelling under their clothes, Jayden backed Maxwell to the wall. They pressed themselves to each other, holding their faces as they kissed greedily.

It was Jayden who pulled away, his breath ragged. He leaned in anew for more of Maxwell's mouth, which Maxwell let him claim without argument. Then Jayden pushed away again. He took a step back.

'I'll talk to Kai.'

Maxwell nodded, breathless. He thought the mention of Kai would put him off, but he wanted Jayden so much. He tugged on Jayden's arms, pulling him back to him. He realised if he gave in, then he was going back on what he needed from Jayden about Kai knowing about them.

He put a hand between his and Jayden's mouths, letting out an aroused and discouraged moan. Leaning his head against the wall, Maxwell inhaled deeply a few times, trying to catch his breath.

'Okay, talk to Kai.'

He and Jayden held each other a while longer, resisting their immediate urges and needs while breathing spasmically, as the intensity of their desire made them feel each other so deeply on an emotional level.

Then Jayden backed away and left.

CHAPTER 6

Jayden returned to see Kai after his physio. It had gone well, all things considered. His legs were still mushy, but in a month's time, the doctors believed Kai would be walking out of the hospital with either a walker or a cane.

Getting his lower body to respond was key right now, and Kai would have to continue to exercise his muscles for several months to regain full capacity of them.

'That's amazing news, Kai!' Jayden beamed at him, yet his gaze remained distant, and Kai could only guess why.

Kai took Jayden's hand and interlaced their fingers. 'I'm amazed you still love me, Jayden.'

'I could never stop loving you.' Jayden hesitated. 'We were going to promise the rest of our lives to each other. Of course, I would still love you now.'

'You know what I mean, Jayden,' said Kai, tilting his head to the side. 'I was as good as dead for three years. And even if you . . . found someone, you still love me, and that . . . it's what's making all this that little bit easier.'

It was true, knowing he had Jayden made the struggles Kai was experiencing now and the shock of readjustment seem worth it.

Jayden got that apologetic look on his face. 'I feel so guilty that I . . . also love someone else.'

Kai winced internally. 'Don't, I get it. I was out for three years. That you still love me despite falling for another man, that amazes me.' Kai repeated so that Jayden would know he meant what he said. 'And I'm so grateful you told me the truth as soon as. You have no idea how much that means to me.'

Kai was responsible for why he was out that night. 'Had I not been out there . . .' And Kai knew the real reason he had stepped out that night.

Jayden and Kai shared a silent moment where neither of them dared speak what they truly wished to express. Instead, Kai guessed at what was on Jayden's mind.

'You want to keep seeing him?' Kai asked.

Jayden bowed his head. 'I . . . yes.'

'Okay.'

Jayden stared at Kai, stunned. 'Okay? No protests, no—'

'Jayden, I get.' Kai cupped his fiancé's cheek. 'I don't have to like it, but I am not angry about it. Hurt, yes, but angry? How *can* I be? I'm the one who decided to . . . step out.'

'You keep saying that,' noted Jayden.

'All I'm saying is . . . if I can have you too, then . . . we can explore a polyamorous relationship. I'm . . . open to that idea.'

Kai's heart sank as he saw the smile on Jayden's face and the twinkle in his green eyes. All Kai wanted was to make Jayden happy. He *was* willing to do this, for Jayden, and perhaps part of him felt like he owed it to Jayden, for he too felt guilty. If only Kai had resisted that one mistake. He had barely left the apartment, but he had left all the same.

Jayden brought Kai's hand to his mouth and kissed it. 'Thank you for understanding,' he whispered.

* * *

Part of Maxwell was relieved to hear Jayden would continue to see him, the other part of him was jealous that he had to share him with Kai. Then again, none of them would be in this mess if it hadn't been for Maxwell. Or perhaps the only person to blame for all this was Daryl and his ability to appear sober when drunk off his ass.

Maxwell missed the guy – he had been a good friend. Maxwell had gone to see him in prison a good number of times, but they grew apart, given the circumstances. Daryl would do his time – he knew he screwed up, that was why he had pled guilty. He took it as a sign to sober up, clean up his act, and when he got out, he would never drink a sip again, never drive again.

Daryl had claimed he wanted to open up his own rehab centre. Big ambitions for a changing man, but his heart had always been in the right place. He wasn't a bad person, none of them were, they were all just flawed.

Maxwell picked up a small bouquet, hoping it would be sufficient to garner at least a moment to apologise.

He strode up to Kai's room and hesitated. He had not told Jayden he would be visiting. What was Kai to Maxwell now? His boyfriend's fiancé? Maxwell was uncertain whether he should introduce himself as the man who had slept with Kai's fiancé or the man who had swerved a car on top of him.

Maxwell slowly entered the room and saw that it was empty. Partly relieved, Maxwell turned and walked back the way he came, holding the bouquet low at his side.

Maxwell turned a corner to see the young man with a walker being helped by a nurse as he sludged along, trying to carry his legs but only managing to push forward with his arms and drag his feet through sheer upper body strength.

Maxwell froze. The pressure on his chest kept throbbing. *He* had caused this.

Kai looked up and his jaw dropped.

Maxwell chickened out. He spun around and began the other way with hurried steps.

'Wait!' Kai called out. 'Please wait!'

Maxwell kept apace.

'I forgive you!'

Maxwell stopped. He turned to look at Kai who, helped by the nurse, came closer. Kai sat down on the walker's bench.

'What do you forgive me for?' Maxwell asked carefully.

'For the accident.' Kai studied Maxwell. 'One of the first things I remembered upon waking up was your face. And seeing it now, I know you've been haunted by what happened all these years.'

Maxwell closed his eyes. 'You have no idea how much I tried to punish myself for my mistake.'

'I saw what you did to save that family,' said Kai. 'How can I fault you for saving lives?'

Maxwell looked back at Kai. 'I failed to save you. I've been trying to save you for three years. I only learnt you were alive recently.' Kai acknowledged in a way that told Maxwell he understood the meaning of his words.

Kai tried to stand but failed. Maxwell caught him by the underarms. 'I've got you.'

The nurse came over to help out. Kai held tightly to Maxwell's arms. He peered into his eyes – Jayden had been right, those blue eyes were mesmerising.

'I am going to be fine,' Kai asserted. 'I am alive and my muscles are going to recover in time.' Kai smiled. 'I've been given a second chance, and that with the man I love.'

Maxwell swallowed his guilt.

Kai winced. 'Even if I have to share him, now that he's gone and fallen in love with another man.'

'Yeah, sorry. Look, I just need to say it, Kai.' Maxwell continued to hold Kai, and continued to hold his gaze. 'I'm sorry for what I did to you.'

'I forgive you,' Kai repeated, his intense gaze boring deep into Maxwell's soul. A wave of emotions flooded Maxwell and he blinked back the sudden onslaught of tears.

'The times I dreamt about you, reliving the moment, wondering how I could have saved you too. I never once stopped thinking about you, Kai, even while I never knew who you were and thought you were dead.'

Kai offered Maxwell a smile. His grip on him was firm, as though Kai was trying to convey unspoken emotions to him.

Clearing his throat, Maxwell helped Kai back onto the seat of his walker. 'I . . . thank you for . . .' That's when it hit him – Kai didn't know Maxwell was the other man. 'These are for you.' Maxwell thrust the flowers in Kai's face.

Kai's smile was warm. 'They're lovely.' He took a beat. 'They gave me your name . . . Maxwell. I hoped I could meet you and tell you I forgive you. Strangely enough, you've been in my dreams and on my mind too.' He winked, and it was such a natural gesture, Maxwell for a moment thought Kai was flirting with him. 'Thank you for coming to see me.'

'You are far too kind, Kai.' Maxwell could see why Jayden loved this man so much.

'You're him, aren't you? Jayden's other man?' Maxwell stood dumbfounded for a moment. Kai pointed, 'Same name.'

'Listen, I . . .' Maxwell fidgeted. 'I had no idea . . .' He motioned between them. 'Not until more recently.'

Kai's eyes grew misty. 'Thank you for saving my fiancé's life that night. And . . .' He looked away. 'Jayden must've told you we agreed to exploring a poly relationship, now that you're in our lives. I'm grateful Jayden has someone. I doubt you're keen to share him, and honestly, neither am I, but I'm willing to try this for him – because I love him. I want to see him happy, and I want to be with him.'

Kai's honesty tugged at Maxwell's heart. Kai deserved Maxwell's honesty as well.

'Kai, I have fallen in love with Jayden and I want to be with him.' Kai nodded. Maxwell added, 'I want to respect you in this too.'

Kai looked up at Maxwell, a soft smile upon his face. 'Then go take care of my fiancé while I cannot.'

Kai held out his hand to Maxwell. Maxwell shook it.

'I am doing this for Jayden,' said Kai.

'So am I,' replied Maxwell.

An understanding passed between them, their love for Jayden perhaps the only thing allowing that to happen.

'Crazy how life wound up and brought us all together,' voiced Kai. Maxwell let out a small laugh. Kai brought the flowers to his nose, this time, his smile turned into a flattered grin, his cheeks reddening. 'Thank you again for these, Maxwell.'

'It's a poor substitute for everything I owe you—'

'You're just as bad as Jayden,' laughed Kai. He sobered. 'Accept that I've accepted your apology.'

'Okay.' Maxwell backed away.

Kai quickly became forlorn again. He must have noticed the sympathy on Maxwell's face, for he rolled his eyes and dismissed him with a shooing motion. Maxwell took his cue and left, grateful and regretful.

CHAPTER 7

A few weeks passed, Jayden had assisted with Kai's physio. Parts of Kai's lower body still weren't responding as Kai had hoped.

It was strange how circumstances had un-folded. Kai and Jayden had argued about Maxwell.

'Why didn't you tell me he was the same guy who landed me in a coma?'

Kai hadn't been angry, but disappointed that Jayden had left out that important detail, which Kai had had to deduce himself after searching the name of the man who inadvertently hit him with the car.

Kai truly did not blame Maxwell for the accident. Kai knew why he'd been out there, and Kai had seen Maxwell swerve away from that family. And Kai had seen Maxwell's horrified expression when he realised Kai was where he had directed the car.

Maxwell had stopped Kai from making a terrible mistake that might have cost him his future with Jayden. So, despite everything, how *could* he hate Maxwell?

Jayden sat on the edge of the bed. The nurse had closed the drapes around Kai's bed. He was in a private room, but this gave them more privacy to make out.

Kai enjoyed their moments together like this.

Jayden cupped Kai's face and kissed him tenderly, Kai deepened the kiss and let out a groan as he felt his body twitch and react. He gasped.

'Jayden!' He took his fiancé's hand and guided it to his crotch. 'My lower body is responding.'

Kai stared into Jayden's green eyes, which darkened with desire. Claiming Kai's lips in a feverish kiss, Jayden moved to straddle Kai and reached into his pants. Kai could barely contain himself at the sheer pleasure of the moment and the sensations. He had not been able to feel this since awakening.

Breathing heavily and pressing their lips together to keep quiet, Kai and Jayden made love in the hospital bed for the first time in three years, for the first time since Kai woke up.

Both of them wept heavily afterwards, sweating and holding each other tightly as they relished this moment of intimacy between them.

* * *

Maxwell tossed his phone onto the couch and passed his hand through his hair. Checking his phone every minute was not going to make Jayden call him. Maxwell wanted to give Jayden and Kai their space this week. Kai was returning home.

At the same time, Maxwell desperately wanted to hear from Jayden.

A knock at the door jolted him from his pining. Maxwell answered to find Kai leaning on a quad cane on the other side of the threshold.

'Hello, Maxwell. Can I come in?'

'Uh, sure.' Maxwell swallowed as Kai shuffled past him, struggling but able to walk and able to stand, which was a huge improvement to how Maxwell had last seen him.

'Can I get you anything to drink?' Maxwell began listing the juices he had, the kinds of tea. Kai dismissed the offer.

'You must be wondering why I'm here,' said Kai.

'Frankly, yes.'

Kai offered him a lopsided smile. 'I want to know the man my fiancé fell in love with.' His eyes travelled the length of Maxwell's body. 'I mean, I can see the appeal, and' – he pointed a thumb over his shoulder – 'bringing me flowers at the hospital?'

Kai shuffled over to the couch and plopped down, setting his cane aside. Maxwell joined him.

'Jayden doesn't talk much about you to me. I think he's trying to protect me from feeling hurt or jealous. But if we're doing this, *really* doing this – you and me sharing Jayden – then I want to know you, beyond you feeling guilty for what happened and you saving Jayden from himself. I want to know who Maxwell is.'

Maxwell tried to read Kai, tried to decipher his angle, but all he could perceive was genuine curiosity, and an earnest need to understand why the man he loved had fallen for another man – *this* other man.

'All right, what do you want to know?' asked Maxwell.

Kai shrugged. 'I know already that you save people, and if by saving you fail somewhere, you are wracked with guilt.'

Maxwell let out a laugh. 'That's an accurate read.'

'Jayden isn't so different from you or me. I think we all have some similar traits. It's probably why we're both so attracted to Jayden, why we fell in love with him.'

'We're not bad men, we're just flawed,' said Maxwell. Kai agreed. 'Jayden doesn't talk much about you either, not since we agreed to be poly. I agree that if we're both going to be part of his life, we should know each other better.'

This seemed to please Kai, for the smile that followed was far more genuine than any Maxwell had seen thus far.

'Can I ask you something, Kai?'

'Anything.'

'Why do you forgive me so readily?' Maxwell observed how Kai's face grew stormy. 'What *were* you doing out there that night?'

Kai bowed his head. 'You're not the only one who needs to be forgiven.'

Maxwell reflexively reached out to take Kai's hand. Kai squeezed back. 'Take your time. If you want to share this with me, I promise to listen without prejudice.'

Maxwell was open and genuine. He was willing to hear the other man out, whatever had led him to be there that night. And whether Maxwell liked it or not, Jayden, and that accident, connected Maxwell and Kai on a level Maxwell couldn't begin to describe.

'Before I met Jayden, there was a guy I kept going back to, an ex. No matter how long we went without speaking to or seeing each other, whenever I saw him, it was like . . . I don't know.' Kai threw his hands up. 'I just can never resist him, we always wind up hooking up.'

Kai put a hand to his brow. 'I cheated on three exes with him, and when I met Jayden, I promised him I would never get in touch with Ron again. But that night, he called me while Jayden was in the shower. He was in town and in a bad way. He needed money.'

Maxwell nodded slowly. Kai paused.

'You have a generous heart,' Maxwell concluded.

Kai shrugged. 'I agreed to meet with him and give him some money. I was on my way to the A.T.M. when it happened.'

Kai looked up at Maxwell, tears in his eyes, and whispered. 'I was going to see my ex in secret, knowing full well what might happen between us, knowing the risks of being in his presence, after promising Jayden I'd never see him again, knowing full well he has a way with me and just uses and discards me, and I still agreed to go see him.'

Maxwell's breath quickened as he began to feel angry, more at the situation than at Kai.

'It's my fault I was there that night, Maxwell. Had I not been, you would have saved four lives and that's it.'

Maxwell looked away. 'That woman testified to paint me a hero.'

'Because you *are*, Maxwell, and you saved me from making a big mistake that night. You stopped me from losing Jayden.'

Maxwell stood abruptly, uncertain to whom his anger was directed.

'This ex of yours, Ron, he's a manipulator,' Maxwell shouted. 'I know folks like that. They pull on your heart-strings, use you for what they want, and then discard you readily. It hurts, and I get it. And he got to you again that night, and you fell for it. And Daryl was drunk because he hadn't yet realised he needed rehab. He lied, and I swerved, and all this – me, you, we . . . Jayden.'

Maxwell slumped back down on the couch. 'What a mess everything is.'

After a beat, Kai spoke again. 'That is what I need to be forgiven for.'

Maxwell met his gaze, 'Jayden needs to know – he *deserves* to know. But for what it's worth, Kai, I am not angry at you for being in my path, nor for being in my life in this way.'

As though Maxwell had unleashed a dam, Kai broke into sobs. Maxwell reflexively wrapped his arms around him, stroking his back. Maxwell couldn't help wanting to save people, wanting to comfort them.

Kai pulled away, steadying his breath, and took his phone out. 'Jayden, I went to see Maxwell. Can you come over?'

'Yeah, sure.'

Kai put his phone away and grabbed his cane, leaning his hands on it and his head on his hands. 'It's done. Jayden will know the full truth of that night.'

* * *

Jayden gaped at Kai in disbelief. 'You were going to see *him?* After promising you wouldn't and knowing full well you can't control yourself around him?'

'I know, I'm so sorry.'

Jayden pulled at his hair and Kai tried to walk over to him with difficulty as his muscles still felt like lead.

'And you told *Maxwell* before telling *me?*'

'I just listened,' Maxwell protested.

'Do *either of you* realise that both of you are the reason all this happened?' hissed Jayden. 'That *both of you* are the reason I kept doing *this*— to myself?' He pulled up his sleeve.

Maxwell winced. Kai could only guess he was imagining finding Jayden in a pool of his blood. Kai couldn't blame Jayden for his vehement outburst, it had been a long time coming.

Kai put a hand to his chest. 'It hurts, it clenches. I feel it in here. Jayden, please forgive me. But Maxwell stopped all that. Despite what happened, he stopped me from losing you. And thanks to his understanding, I still have you.' He paused. 'Do I?'

Jayden shouted in anger, pacing before stopping abruptly. When he spoke, his voice shook, and tears streamed down his cheeks. 'I don't know if I want you both in my life or out of it right now!'

'Me? But I . . .'

'Stop it, Maxwell. You contributed, inadvertently. But you still are a part of this mess as much as Kai and I are. The three of us are in this whether we like it or not, and right now, this is just a lot to take in. I felt guilty, I blamed myself, but it was *your* fault,' he pointed at Kai, '*and* yours,' he pointed at Maxwell, 'that I have been suffering for three years. You don't think I feel it in my gut either?'

Maxwell turned a pained face away, tears falling from his eyes. 'I feel it physically some days, hit after hit, and I regret it every day.'

Jayden sighed, wiping his eyes. 'I need some time on my own.'

'Then I'll come home a little later,' said Kai.

'No, Kai – I need to be left alone for a while – days, weeks, I don't know. I need to process all this. I need to figure out what you both mean to me. I don't like blaming you, and up until now, I wasn't. I need a clear head. I need to assess whether I still want you both in my life in light of this new information.'

Jayden slammed the door on his way out. Kai called out his name, unable to go after him, wanting Maxwell to pursue him, but the other man merely pressed a hand to his mouth, weeping.

'I'm sorry, Kai. I didn't think he would react like that. I, uh . . .' Maxwell looked around. 'You can stay here, and I'll go pick up your things, whatever you might need, from Jayden's place . . . well, your place.'

'Okay, thanks.' Kai nodded, as reality sank in and as his stomach sank.

'We've lost him!' Maxwell heaved.

Kai put an arm around Maxwell, using all his strength to remain on his feet when he just wanted to crumble.

'How could it have come to this?' Maxwell quavered.

Kai could no longer support himself, let alone the bigger man, and he collapsed to the floor. Maxwell lifted him immediately before he could fall completely. He brought him to the couch where both of them crumpled.

And then, without another word, both leaned on each other, letting their tears fall.

CHAPTER 8

Maxwell sent another message. No response. He shook his head as Kai looked over expectantly.

Finally, his phone rang. Jayden sounded more annoyed than anything else, but it was a relief all the same to hear his voice. Maxwell put him on speaker.

'You can stop freaking out that I'm going to hurt myself. I just need my space, okay?'

'And we get it,' said Maxwell. 'We just worry about you. We love you.'

Jayden sighed. 'Look, I can call you to check in and let you know I'm fine, but I need you both to respect where I'm at right now.'

'We do, we will,' said Kai.

And that was that.

Several weeks passed, where Kai stayed at Maxwell's. Maxwell drove him to his physio and helped him with his home exercises. Jayden called every few days to let them know he was fine and to catch up sometimes, but none of them had spoken about what truly mattered.

Kai glanced up from his yoga mat at Maxwell. The Japanese man's hair fanned out on the mat.

'Stop messaging him. Jayden's going to think we're both obsessed, and we both know – you and I – that *you* are the obsessed one of us two.'

That got a chuckle out of Maxwell. He joined Kai on the floor, lying down beside him.

'To say these are weird circumstances is an understatement,' said Maxwell.

'Whatever our circumstances, I still need to do my exercises.'

Kai brought one knee in, holding it into a stretch. 'I can get it closer now.'

'That's awesome!' Maxwell bent his knee. He cried out. 'Damn, how do you do this? I feel like this stretch is making me discover muscles I never knew I had.'

Kai laughed. He turned his head to Maxwell as both remained on their backs, side by side. 'Can I ask you something?'

'Anything.'

Kai hesitated but a moment – there was a glint in his eyes that made Maxwell's heart palpitate. 'Did I really haunt your dreams?'

That took Maxwell by surprise. 'Yeah, you did. I couldn't stop thinking about you. Your face was all I saw every night.' Maxwell stared deep into Kai's blue eyes. 'Sometimes it still is.'

Kai probed Maxwell's face with his eyes, his expression inscrutable. 'When I woke up, the first person I thought of, the first face I saw, it wasn't Jayden. It was you.'

Something in Maxwell's chest squeezed and fluttered. He turned to stare up at the ceiling to stop the urge to kiss Kai.

Maxwell sighed. 'Bicycle?'

'Bicycle.'

The two began counting out loud as they lifted their legs for the air cycling exercise. After fifty, they stopped. Maxwell's heart continued to race.

'You're getting good at this.' Maxwell pointed out, trying to sound casual. 'Another accomplishment in your recovery, my friend.'

Kai chuckled, turning his head to look at Maxwell again.

Then, Kai rolled on top of him and claimed his lips. And Maxwell reciprocated, wrapping his arms around Kai, sucking in his tongue.

Kai pushed himself off, rolling onto his back. 'I'm sorry.' Kai got to his feet, if a bit shakily.

Maxwell stood as well. '*I'm* not.' Maxwell let out a small laugh. 'I am sorry for so many things but not this.'

Kai stepped up to him. Maxwell clocked how stronger Kai was now without his cane. 'I can see why Jayden fell in love with you, Maxwell. You're kind, caring, attentive. You put the needs of others before yours, and yet you're not afraid to assert what *you* need.'

Kai lifted his hand and caressed Maxwell's face. 'And Jayden might not be the only one in this triangle to have fallen for you.'

Maxwell lunged for Kai's lips, grabbing his face with both hands. Kai moaned, and Maxwell felt Kai melt in his embrace as the two devoured each other.

Maxwell took Kai by the thighs, lifting him as Kai wrapped his legs around him. Backing him up to the wall, Maxwell pressed himself against Kai. Both paused only long enough to whisper each other's names before plunging back in for more of each other.

Maxwell carried Kai to the bed atop which the two fell, sliding up and down each other. Maxwell wanted to laugh at how much he wanted Kai right now, and he could see the lust in the other man's eyes. He reached under Kai's shirt as Kai reached for Maxwell's belt.

Maxwell's phone rang. He ignored it. But then it occurred to him that it might be Jayden. He could see by how Kai paused that he was thinking the same thing.

'Fuck!' hissed Maxwell.

He grabbed his phone and indeed it was Jayden.

'You have to answer it,' said Kai, panting.

Straddling Kai, Maxwell straightened and answered his phone, putting Jayden on speaker like he always did when Jayden called them.

'Jayden, hi!'

'You sound out of breath. You two having sex now or what?' The question was a joke, but enough to sound like a genuine concern that had crossed Jayden's mind.

Both Maxwell and Kai defended their breathiness.

'We were doing exercises!'

'Going through Kai's regimen!'

They paused and Jayden was silent. Kai's eyes widened and Maxwell's stomach clenched, realising they sounded far too guilty.

'Oh my god, un-fucking-believable. You were totally having sex, weren't you? And don't lie to me!'

'We're still dressed,' protested Maxwell.

'In our defence,' began Kai, glaring and scowling at Maxwell who winced at his own stupid reply, 'we agreed to have a polyamorous relationship. Now how is it you get to be the only one we get to be with and have to share? Maxwell and I are simply being polyamorous right now.'

'I think it's time we had a proper chat, all three of us. I'm coming over.' Jayden hung up.

Maxwell stared down at Kai, still out of breath.

'We're still dressed?' chided Kai.

'I know!' Maxwell fell onto his back beside Kai. 'It was a stupid response.'

'We're not doing anything wrong. We both agreed to share Jayden, and we both agreed to polyamory. So if you and I hook up, I mean . . . well, I suppose that's why we need to sort this out once and for all.'

Kai looked at Maxwell. 'Maxwell, I love Jayden and I also want you.'

'I realise I want you too, Kai, in case you hadn't noticed.' Maxwell pointed at his still bulging groin. 'I just hope we haven't lost Jayden. I love him so much.'

Kai interlaced his hand with Maxwell's. 'I love him so deeply.'

Maxwell sighed. 'I was lying on this very side of Jayden's bed when the hospital rang. It was the first time Jayden and I stopped resisting each other, the first time we made love. And then you woke up.'

'To be fair, I'd been awake for hours already. It just took that long for them to examine me and ensure I was mentally clear, what with my miraculous groggy yet full mind and memory.'

'Kai, your survival and recovery are phenomenal. It's amazing. For what it's worth, I'm glad you survived, for many reasons.'

'For what it's worth, I'm glad we crossed paths. I appreciate you in my life, Maxwell, in all the ways you encountered me.'

The two lay there for a while more before getting up and settling on the couch while they waited for Jayden to arrive.

* * *

Jayden was uncertain if he would be interrupting anything when he lifted his fist to knock on the door. He wasn't sure what the pang he felt was. Jealousy for one or the other, or for both?

Kai was right, they had agreed to polyamory. Kai and Maxwell had done nothing wrong. Jayden had been with both of them for months now. Now Kai and Maxwell were hooking up? Perhaps this was what it had always been supposed to be for the three of them.

Jayden knocked and opened the door himself. Both Kai and Maxwell stood from the couch, taking a step forward. Jayden stopped as both men stared agape, their eyes pleading.

'Jayden,' they both whispered. It was so perfect, both their voice timbres resonating so well together.

'Before you say anything,' began Kai, 'I want you to know how much I love you. I want to spend the rest of my life with you. That has not changed. It never will.'

Maxwell's jaw set the way it did when something pained him. 'I love you, Jayden,' he said softly.

'Tell us there's a way to move past this,' Kai implored.

'We want each other,' said Maxwell.

Jayden nodded. 'We do.' Jayden entered properly, joining the two in the living room. 'I want you. I need you. I love you. Both of you.'

Maxwell passed a hand through his hair, groaning in frustration. 'Argh, this is so messed up. I have *never* felt this way about two people at the same time before, let alone . . .' He sighed.

'Neither have I,' admitted Jayden.

'I've gone and fallen in love with the same man my fiancé has.'

Maxwell's face twitched. Jayden could tell he had felt Kai's words physically, much like Jayden would feel Kai or Maxwell physically – their words, the thought of them.

For a moment, all three gaped at one another before a series of chuckles escaped them.

'This is way weird, beyond weird,' voiced Jayden. Sobering, he met his lovers' gazes. 'Did you have sex? I just want the truth.'

'We stopped, you interrupted,' Maxwell answered quickly. 'We were going to, but it wouldn't have just been sex.'

Jayden nodded, understanding. 'We want each other,' he repeated with even more conviction. 'All of us. I love you both. I don't think I can choose.'

'I don't want to share you,' said Maxwell. 'The thought of it makes me feel . . .'

'Lonely.' It was Jayden who completed. That was how he had felt when he realised Maxwell and Kai had feelings for each other and he had been the one to push them together. Or had he?

'Maybe we don't have to so much share as be shared.' Jayden and Maxwell turned to Kai, who continued. 'It's obvious to me what the three of us need, with how we feel about each other. What if we chose to be poly together? Then we wouldn't be seeing one or the other or sharing, we would all be, the three of us, invested in a relationship.'

'Fate did seem to bring us together in this strange way,' added Jayden.

Maxwell shook his head. 'I don't deserve either of you.'

'You aren't at fault, Maxwell,' insisted Kai. 'I played a part that night too. The only true innocent one among us is Jayden.'

'Had it not been for me, though, you'd be married, almost three years in,' protested Maxwell, his voice rising.

'You don't know that,' argued Kai.

'Blame Daryl,' shouted Jayden. 'Not yourself.'

Jayden grabbed Maxwell's forearm. 'You think I never noticed your scars, just because they're older and cleaner than mine? You've punished yourself enough for the accident that wasn't your fault.'

Maxwell's eyes brimmed with tears.

Jayden placed a hand on his cheek. 'I agree if we all invest in each other, we won't be sharing or shared, we'll be together, tending to each other's needs. If we're together, we can be there for each other whenever we need each other. We can support each other in ways we might not be able to otherwise. Each of us can bring something to this relationship that we each need.'

'And then Jayden can be with both of us. I can be with both of you, you can be–'

'Yes, I get it, but I caused you both such turmoil.'

'Maxwell,' Kai cupped his other cheek. 'I've fallen in love with you. I want to be with you as much as I want to be with Jayden. I want you.'

'I want to be with you too, Maxwell,' said Jayden.

'I deserve for you both to cut me out of your lives,' Maxwell seethed, the same way he had at the hospital.

'You never stopped punishing yourself, Maxwell. This is just how you're doing it now.' Jayden said it so matter-of-factly, never taking his hand off Maxwell's face.

Jayden's words seemed to hit Maxwell deeply, as he reflexively brought a hand to his arm, rubbing it and hugging it.

'I keep feeling that without me, none of this would have happened,' whispered Maxwell.

'Then I would have never met you,' said Kai, 'and my life is a whole lot better with you in it. You stopped me from making a terrible mistake. We have all been brought together again because there is more between us, and there always would have been.' Kai furrowed his brows. 'Maxwell, you and I were linked that night, and our hearts yearned for each other in the only manner we would understand at that time. But they were linked, and we were brought together. I would have always sought you out once I awoke.'

Maxwell remained silent, his focus darting between Kai and Jayden, then settling on Jayden. 'And you?'

'The only man who made me feel anything aside from Kai is you, Maxwell.'

Maxwell's eyes were so earnest, it tugged at Jayden. Jayden wanted him so much in that moment, and the way Kai looked on, so hopeful for them to make this work, Jayden wanted Kai so much too.

'I said yes to Kai when he asked me to spend the rest of my life with him,' said Jayden, 'and now I'm asking you to be a part of this, to be a part of us.'

Jayden waited, giving Maxwell the time he needed to allow their words to resonate in his heart. Jayden didn't know how he would cope if Maxwell said no. Jayden would have Kai, but without Maxwell, he would feel incomplete and unfulfilled. Maxwell had always been the missing piece, even before Jayden and Kai knew a piece to their hearts was missing.

'Yes, I accept,' Maxwell said finally. The relief Jayden felt was instant. 'I want and need you both too,' Maxwell declared. 'I love you both too.'

Jayden pulled both of them into an embrace. He kissed Maxwell's cheek, as did Kai. His stomach flipping and whooping, and oscillating between joy and trepidation, Jayden took Maxwell's face with both hands and pressed a hard kiss to him, wanting to convey his commitment.

Jayden then turned to Kai, who claimed his lips before Jayden watched Kai and Maxwell exchange a kiss that, before, might have made Jayden feel jealous, but now made him feel something that gave him hope for their future.

The three of them continued this exchange of kisses, alternating and kissing together, three tongues twining fervently.

'I want you both right now,' Jayden expressed. And his desire was reciprocated by both.

Interlacing his hands with both Jayden and Kai, Maxwell led them to his bedroom, where they, at first awkwardly and tentatively, explored each other as a trio, before making exhilarating love. The best of all three for each other, attentively taking care in the way that they pleasured each other. The sensation of feeling the love and want from both of them at the same time was so elating, Jayden had never before felt this euphoric during sex or this satisfied.

Jayden voiced his feelings once they had come down from their orgasms and lay on the bed together, Jayden between Maxwell and Kai. Both had their arms wrapped around Jayden and each other.

'It's as though each of you fulfils a need the other cannot, and emotionally too, I can feel that so deeply.'

'I know what you mean, baby,' said Kai.

'I felt it too,' said Maxwell. 'Like something that was missing no longer is, now that it's the three of us.'

Something inside Jayden released. He no longer felt suffocated, not even while his heart clenched and unclenched still from all the emotions they had all shared over the past months.

'Look, I know we still have a lot to figure out between us,' said Jayden, reiterating his desires, 'but I want us to be together, all three of us.'

Kai looked from Jayden to Maxwell, hopeful. 'I want that too.'

'As do I,' said Maxwell without taking a beat.

It filled Jayden's heart with warmth to know the two men he loved, loved him enough to give this a real go.

Jayden voiced softly, 'I want us to love each other.'

Kai smiled, interlacing each of his hands with Jayden's and Maxwell's. 'I want us to heal together.'

Maxwell blinked a few times, his eyes red. He interlaced his free hand with Jayden's other hand, 'I want us to forgive each other.'

Jayden's breath caught in his throat with emotions.

The three of them, with silent tears, wrapped their interlaced arms around each other, twining their legs together, and they closed their eyes, allowing their emotions to flow freely.

Trinity of Affection

One year following Jayden, Kai, and Maxwell's declarations of love and commitment to a polyamorous relationship, the three now face new challenges as they plan their wedding.

Maxwell visits Daryl in prison, the estranged friend who caused the accident that put Kai in a coma four years prior, Jayden has yet to forgive Daryl for all that transpired, and Kai faces someone from his past who could put the whole polyamorous relationship in jeopardy.

Chapter 1

Maxwell sat facing Daryl in the visitor's hall of the prison, his heart thumping nervously. He had not seen his friend in over a year. The blond jock was beaming, but Maxwell could see the hurt in his friend's pale blue eyes.

'It's been so long, man!' Daryl's smile never faltered and it tugged at Maxwell's heart.

'I'm sorry,' was all Maxwell could say.

'So . . . is there a reason you haven't come to see me in, like, a year?' Daryl folded his muscular arms, leaning back. 'Had you not sent me that letter six months ago, I . . .' Daryl chewed his lip nervously. He muttered, hurt seeping into his voice, 'I thought you'd done something to yourself.'

'Shit, Daryl, man, I'm so sorry.' Maxwell felt devastated. 'I haven't done anything to myself in a long time.'

Daryl nodded. 'You used to come regularly, I just . . .' Daryl smiled again. 'So what brings you here now?'

'I'm getting married,' said Maxwell.

Daryl's eyes widened. 'Wow, congrats, man. Who's the lucky fella?'

'Two of them, actually. I'm in a polyamorous relationship.'

Daryl let out a low whistle. 'How does that work?'

'Well, the three of us share a king-sized bed,' began Maxwell.

'Not what I was referring to.'

'Sorry.' Maxwell chuckled, blushing. 'We're still trying to figure out the finer points of it all.'

Maxwell thought back to the night Kai and Jayden proposed to him. They had been reiterating that they renewed their engagement, and then as Maxwell's heart had sunk, they both went down on one knee, holding up an engagement ring and asked, 'Will you marry us?'

The three of them had been living together since they committed to their poly relationship prior to all this. The proposal had made Maxwell's heart soar. Maxwell, Jayden and Kai had been together a year now, officially.

'We're going to wait another year before the big day,' explained Maxwell. 'And that's why I'm here. I'd like you to be my best man.'

Daryl blinked a few times, and then his face changed. There it was, the anger being let out.

'What the fuck? You leave me high and dry and stop coming to visit me for a whole year? And now you want me to be your best man? No explanation as to why you . . . forgot about me!'

'I didn't forget about you, Daryl.'

'I thought something bad had happened, I thought you resented me. Like, I made a mistake, I've cleaned my act, and I'm gonna get out next year a changed man. I got no choice, I'm . . .' Daryl sighed. 'Brigitte came to see me.'

'Your ex?'

'Yeah. Max, I'm . . . I'm a dad.'

'What?' It was Maxwell's turn to gape, wide-eyed.

'Brigitte said she found out after the accident that she was pregnant. She finally came to tell me and she swears the kid knows that daddy made a mistake and "got sent to detention" for a few years. She wants to bring him next time. He's three.'

'Congratulations, Daryl. That's amazing! Any chance you and she might . . .?'

'Nah, she's got a new man. I just feel blessed I get to be in my kid's life.' Daryl offered Maxwell a wan smile. 'I get it, you've been navigating your poly relationship. Just, it would've been nice to hear from you sooner.'

'I know.'

Daryl smirked. 'So who are the two men?'

The question Maxwell was trying to avoid answering knowing he had to tell him today.

'Well, there's Jayden. I met him first, kind of. At work.'

'Ooh, office romance. All right, and the other?'

As Maxwell stared at Daryl, his friend's face changed to a grim expression that probably matched Maxwell's.

'Kai Nakagawa.'

It took Daryl a moment before he schooled his expression of shock. 'He's alive? Do you know who that is, Maxwell?'

'Yes. I know now. When I met Jayden, I did not, but . . . Kai was Jayden's fiancé when the accident happened. Kai knows too. He knows I'm the one who put him in a coma.'

'Law says *I* did that.' Daryl was pensive. 'So that's why I haven't heard from you. Because you were dating the reason I'm in here.'

Maxwell bowed his head. 'Yeah. I, uh, would like you to meet them.' He cast a hopeful glance at Daryl who only stared wide-eyed. 'He's forgiven you, by the way. *And* me, obviously.'

'I don't mind meeting them. But can I think about it, about being your best man? I want to say yes, but given the circumstances . . .'

Maxwell felt dismayed but understood. 'Of course.'

'Thanks.'

The silence that followed was awkward. Thankfully, time was up for visitors and Maxwell was relieved to be stepping out of that room. He perceived Daryl was too. Maxwell owed him a few more apologies.

* * *

Jayden jumped up onto the safe in one bound, his excitement pumping him with so much energy. His fiancés waited for him to make his announcement.

'Okay, so I've got the solution to the legal issue.'

A smirk played at the corner of Maxwell's mouth. 'Let me guess, we move to a different country where we can marry more than one person?'

Jayden rolled his eyes, exaggerating the roll of his neck, and nearly fell off the couch.

'Easy there.' Chuckling, Maxwell put up his hand to steady him.

Kai remained pensive. 'I know I'm the one who proposed to Jayden first, but if the two of you are intent on being legally married, I don't mind being the additional spouse.'

'That isn't fair on you,' protested Maxwell. 'I was third into the relationship, therefore I should be—'

'You are not third!' Kai scolded. 'Maxwell, darling, you are equally part of this relationship. Not a third into it, not a third wheel. We are three, we are a trinity, and you and your needs matter just as much. I did not want to marry Jayden without you. The moment I realised I was in love with you, I knew, if I married Jayden, it had to be with you. To marry you both.'

'And I love you as much to want to marry you both too – that's why I said yes.'

'And me three. Now will the two of you stop bickering and just listen?' Jayden made a face, chiding them with his eyes.

Both Maxwell and Kai opened their mouths to protest, but Jayden clamped his hands on both their mouths. He smiled, satisfied with himself.

'We are equal in this relationship, and none of us want the other to be left out, and we're all willing to . . .' He thought about it. 'Sacrifice ourselves, as it were. So?' Jayden grinned. 'None of us marry legally.'

Both his fiancés scowled – their voices as they queried further were muffled by Jayden's hands. 'Instead, we remain common-law spouses, *but* . . . we sign a *symbolic* document, one that can be legally binding to us *three*, but isn't a marriage contract as it is in the law. It is for us, to us, to promise each other to live like married husbands.'

Jayden saw his fiancés consider it thoughtfully. He went on. 'It will be as legal as it can be, like a business contract, more, I think, but . . .' Jayden let go of his fiancés' mouths, losing his balance and stepped down from the sofa. 'It will be *our* contract, it will mean something to *us*. Our partnership, our relationship, our promises to each other, binding our love and our vows.'

Jayden waited.

Maxwell and Kai broke into grins.

'That's actually not such a bad idea,' voiced Maxwell.

'I'm down for that. I know a good lawyer – I am certain she can find something close to what we want that can represent our intent well.'

'I have no doubt your sister will be able to produce exactly what we need, Kai.' Jayden was overjoyed. And he realised, relieved. He sighed loudly. 'I am so happy the two of you like my idea.'

Both of them wrapped their arms around him.

'Of course, babe.' Kai kissed Jayden's cheek. 'We love your idea . . . because we love you.'

'And if either of you have questions, concerns, any-thing,' began Jayden.

'We'll be honest and talk about it, the three of us,' Maxwell reassured.

Jayden nodded, closing his eyes and leaning into the tri-embrace. He *was* reassured. They were figuring it out. That was what mattered most to him right now.

CHAPTER 2

The day had come for all three of them to visit Daryl in prison. Kai was so nervous, he needed to release the tension. Jayden had gone out to run some errands. Kai claimed Maxwell for a tender moment to unfetter his anxiety. Making love had always been a good way for him to let it all out.

Whether it was with one or the other, or with both of them, Kai continued to be amazed at how he had their love and affection. He would honour the two men with whom he wanted to spend the rest of his life.

Kai had known for a while and had admitted to Jayden that he wanted them both to marry Maxwell. His heart had soared when Jayden had expressed feeling the same way.

True to his promise, Kai had blocked his ex and would never contact him again. He was prepared to call the police should Ron, the ex in question, ever get in touch. Kai wasn't going to jeopardise this beautiful chance he had or hinder his future with the men he loved. He would *honour* them.

Kai and Maxwell made love right there in the hall where they stood, *both* of them needing that release of their anxiety, Kai realised. They both shared the same worry – how would Jayden take meeting Daryl? Jayden had suffered so much, perhaps the most. It was different for all three of them, but Kai and Maxwell knew Jayden had buried something he was not sharing with either of them.

Kai also knew he and Maxwell needed to let Jayden assess his emotions without too much of a push but with just enough of a reminder that they would listen when he was ready to share.

When they reached the prison, the three of them sat facing Daryl, who had joined them when the inmates entered the atrium. Daryl was a handsome man, strongly built, and his square jaw was set as he stared at Kai, clear blue eyes wide, conveying so many un-spoken feelings.

Kai knew Daryl knew who he was.

'Kai . . .' Daryl's voice gave way. The man, for all the fidgeting of his hands and wringing of them, did not look away.

'Hello,' Kai said gently.

Daryl then met Jayden's glare. 'You must be Jayden.'

Jayden put on a fake smile and Kai clocked how Maxwell looked dismayed. This was a lot harder on him than either Kai or Maxwell thought it would be.

'I, uh . . .' Daryl chewed his lip nervously. 'I am so, so, deeply sorry for the pain I caused you.'

Jayden gave a curt nod.

Kai reached for Daryl's hand and looked him deep in the eyes. 'I forgive you, Daryl. For everything.'

Daryl squeezed back, sucking in a sharp breath. He nodded. His eyes never reddened, he was not easily moved by emotion, but Kai could read the relief and sadness in his eyes.

Kai pulled away, smiling tenderly at the man who had brought Maxwell into his life.

'Maxwell tells us you've cleaned up your act,' said Jayden, folding his arms. Kai recognised he was trying to be jovial.

Daryl confirmed. 'I'm never going back to that. I don't want to. I want to help anyone just like me, who has a drinking problem. I'm lucky. I still have my health, my best friend, a son. The bottle? That can go straight in the trash.'

'That is admirable,' said Kai. 'Maxwell told us you were a good man, just flawed, like the rest of us.'

Daryl chuckled. 'Flawed. You can say that again.'

The tension began to ease and everyone relaxed – somewhat.

Daryl smirked. 'You two are perfect for Maxwell. The way you all look at each other?' He let out a laugh. 'Congratulations on your engagement.'

After a bit more chit-chat, it was time to leave. Daryl had asked a favour of Maxwell, who went to visit the mother of Daryl's child, leaving Kai and Jayden alone in the apartment.

'I'm proud of you, baby.' Kai wrapped his arms around Jayden and kissed the nape of his neck.

'I wanted to . . . punch him.'

'Do you want to talk about it?'

Jayden shook his head.

Kai inquired further. 'Do you want to . . . release it?'

Jayden grinned, letting out a small laugh that tugged at Kai's heart in an elating way. 'Depends how you mean that.'

Kai felt his desire bloom. 'In whatever way you want.'

Jayden turned to fully face Kai and backed him towards the bedroom, lunging at him. Kai laughed at Jayden's rough playfulness.

'I am here for you in all the ways your needs need to be met.' Kai expressed.

Jayden paused, sobering. 'I know. And when I'm ready, I'll share.'

'I know.'

Smiling anew, Jayden resumed, and Kai was more than happy to be with him, and be for him all that Jayden needed him to be, to provide, in this moment, all that he desired.

Chapter 3

Jayden paced in the apartment. He was alone. His rage kept mounting. He was angry at himself for feeling the way he was.

He had not forgiven Daryl.

It had been weeks since their visit to the prison. Jayden didn't know if Maxwell would be upset to know.

Jayden was worried the wedding would be called off, that their perfect trio of love would decimate itself, all because Jayden couldn't move past what had happened, what it had caused him to do to himself.

And at that moment, Jayden wanted to hurt himself. Hit himself, cut himself. He had not self-harmed in such a long time now, but the urge was unbearable, the need to punish himself for feeling wrong because of the way he felt.

He leaned against the wall, balling his hands into fists. He scrunched his face, gritting his teeth as tears flowed from his eyes. He screamed his rage out hoarsely.

The door slammed open. Startled Jayden looked up to see Maxwell drop the bags he was carrying. He rushed to Jayden's side and wrapped his arms around him.

Jayden collapsed in Maxwell's arms.

'Jayden, what's going on? What happened?'

Jayden murmured tearfully, 'Please don't hate me.'

'Jayden, I could never hate you – I love you.' Maxwell led Jayden to the couch where he took Jayden's face between his hands and repeated, 'I could never hate you. I love you.'

Maxwell pulled Jayden to him again, stroking his head. 'It's okay. Whatever's happened, it's okay.'

Jayden trembled from sheer fear. 'I . . .' he stammered. 'I haven't forgiven him.'

The tight and tense hold on Jayden that Maxwell had, loosened and he exhaled. His words were far more soothing than Jayden imagined his reaction should be. 'I understand.' Maxwell took a beat. 'Do you need me to uninvite him?'

Jayden pulled away, surprised, staring at Maxwell. 'You would do that for me?'

'Jayden, it's our wedding. The three of us need to feel comfortable. You initially agreed to Daryl's presence for me, but if it's causing you too much hurt, then . . .' Maxwell paused. Jayden could see the turmoil on his face. 'Then yes, I would do that for you.'

Jayden shook his head vigorously. 'No, that's not the solution.'

Kai entered the apartment with more shopping bags and he too immediately dropped those upon seeing Jayden's tearstruck state, and came to sit by Jayden's other side on the couch. His brows creased the way they did when concerned.

'Jayden hasn't forgiven Daryl,' Maxwell explained softly.

'Oh, baby.' Kai kissed Jayden's head.

'I thought you'd hate me, Maxwell. I wanted to hurt myself. The feeling was so strong.'

'I know what that's like, but you did not hurt yourself,' Maxwell soothed.

'I wanted to, though.' Jayden was angry at himself for wanting to hurt himself, and now he wanted to hurt himself for wanting to hurt himself.

'Jayden, not hurting myself doesn't mean I never feel the urge,' said Maxwell. 'It means I manage it better than I used to. That's all. It's okay to experience these urges. It's okay to slip up while we're healing – it's *part* of the healing. And it's okay that you haven't forgiven Daryl.'

'He needs to know,' blurted Jayden. 'I need him to know.'

'Okay.'

Letting out a shaking breath, Jayden leaned back against the couch. Maxwell and Kai followed suit, Kai's arms wrapping around him warmly as Maxwell maintained his embrace. Kai and Maxwell interlaced their fingers together. Each kissed Jayden on the head, then on the cheek. Both whispered simultaneously, 'I love you.'

Jayden chuckled despite himself. 'You'd think the two of you were coordinating your expressions of affection.'

'Maybe we are.' Kai winked at Maxwell.

The two nestled into Jayden on either side of him, and Jayden closed his eyes, relishing the love of his fiancés.

Kai returned to the shopping at some point, to put away what he and Maxwell had brought him, and then went back out to do more, leaving Jayden and Maxwell alone again.

'Do you really not hate me for feeling the way I do?'

Maxwell brushed Jayden's face with the backs of his fingers. 'I love you. I want you to be happy. I am okay with how you feel. My heart clenches because of how hurt you still feel, but we'll do what we need to. Whatever that is.'

Jayden lunged for Maxwell's lips. Maxwell responded in kind, pulling Jayden closer to him for Jayden to straddle him, and the two shared an emotional moment of intimacy, with tears and moans intermingling.

* * *

The three fiancés sat before Daryl who took in the sombre mood. He waited patiently for them to speak.

Jayden began, diving right in. 'I haven't forgiven you.'

Maxwell was so proud of him.

Daryl nodded, as though he had known. 'I get it. And words won't erase what I did.'

Jayden's breath shook. 'No, it won't. Nor what *I* did because of it.' Jayden lifted his sleeve just enough for Daryl to see the scars.

Daryl's face contorted and he clenched his jaw, but he never turned away from the marks on Jayden's arms. 'Kai, I put in a coma; my best friend purposely self-harmed; and so did you.' Daryl raised his head, meeting all their gazes. 'I am *so sorry.*'

Jayden put a hand to his mouth, stifling a sob. Daryl tentatively reached out, then paused. Jayden looked at Daryl's hand as it lingered in the air, the jock hesitating between wanting to comfort and not knowing if he should.

Daryl retracted his hand. Maxwell reached out to take it instead. Daryl gave him the faintest of smiles, letting Maxwell know his appreciation.

An inmate sitting at the table beside theirs began heckling them, making baby cry noises. 'Aw, you gonna cry, princess? Hey Daryl, didn't know you hung out with fa—'

Daryl stood abruptly, taking one large stride towards the inmate, hunkering above him, his pronounced muscles bulging. 'I suggest you shut your mouth, *bigot,* unless you wanna taste the wall when I ram your face in it.'

The security officer stepped in between them, clearing his throat loudly. Daryl withdrew. He pointed behind him. 'My best friend's getting married. And that's a beautiful thing.'

Daryl sat back down. 'Sorry about Steven, he's a real jerk sometimes.'

The three fiancés blinked. Maxwell knew Daryl had his back, always, and that was why the accident had hurt so much, causing a rift he hoped was being mended now.

Jayden let out a chuckle, smiling at Daryl. 'Thanks, I appreciate what you just did.'

'Only what any decent human being should do in the face of such jerks.'

Jayden sighed. 'Look, this doesn't mean I won't ever forgive you or that I don't want you at our wedding.' That filled Maxwell with hope. 'Maxwell wants you there and that means something to me.'

'I confirm I want to be there,' said Daryl. He locked eyes with Maxwell, whose vision blurred momentarily. Kai seemed pleased, and Jayden smiled mildly.

'I want us to move past this. I didn't want to hide it from you . . . this.' Jayden pointed at his arm.

'I get it. Thank you for telling me.' Daryl pressed his lips together, Maxwell knew he was searching for the right thing to say. Finally, Daryl asked, 'What can I do to make amends?'

CHAPTER 4

Jayden stepped out with Kai and Maxwell on either side of him holding his hands. He felt such relief just from expressing his true feelings and opening up to Daryl. He didn't know what Daryl could do to make amends, and that's exactly what he told him. And yet it felt like just hearing Daryl ask it, was enough – for today.

The same way Jayden, Kai and Maxwell had figured things out to be together in a way that worked for all three of them, Jayden knew now, and truly felt, that they would figure things out for him to forgive Daryl so the guy could be Maxwell's best man.

Jayden's joy was so overwhelming, he urged his lovers home so they could embrace this freeing sensation together.

As Jayden shared ebullient intimacy, Jayden realised that Daryl's drunkenness had brought the three of them together in ways they could not have connected otherwise. It wasn't that Jayden was suddenly grateful for what happened, but a heaviness was gone, making way for clarity, and in that clarity, Jayden realised that the true person to blame was not Daryl, nor any of the three of them.

* * *

Maxwell stretched out his arms to relish holding the two men he loved in his embrace. He smiled.

'Thank you,' he whispered. 'For being so amazing. Jayden, for considering forgiving Daryl, and Kai for forgiving him.'

Jayden smiled, as did Kai, but while Jayden's eyes glinted, Kai's merely half-closed. Their smiles were a delight.

Maxwell pressed a kiss to each of their foreheads. 'I'll prepare lunch.'

He attempted to sit up but the other two pulled him back down to pepper him with kisses. Maxwell chuckled. 'Who's coordinated now?'

He grabbed a pillow and flung it at Kai.

'Hey!' the Japanese man protested. As Kai loosened his grip to retaliate, Maxwell sat up and slid towards the foot of the bed – and the pillow hit Jayden.

'Oh my god, Kai!' Jayden grabbed another pillow and playfully bashed Kai with it.

Chuckling proudly to himself, Maxwell stood from the bed as Jayden and Kai continued to battle each other behind him.

Maxwell could hear his lovers argue teasingly as he dressed and began in the kitchen.

'Give me my pants, Kai.'

'Not until you put down that pillow.'

Maxwell called out. 'Behave, you two. Lunch'll be ready soon.'

A knock came at the door, and Maxwell answered. There stood a suave-looking man, leaning against the door frame, smirking enticingly. He was good-looking enough, well-coiffed, but Maxwell had no clue who this guy was.

The man narrowed his eyes. 'Who are you?'

'I could ask you the same. I live here. Who are y—'

'No.'

Jayden had come up behind Maxwell and froze. He balled his hands into fists, face contorting in disdain.

The man scowled at Jayden. 'Who're *you*?'

'Your worst fucking nightmare.'

Jayden grabbed the man by the collar, pulling him into the apartment, and slammed him against the wall, screaming, 'Do you have any idea what you've caused?'

'Whoa, whoa, Jayden, baby.'

Maxwell put his hand on Jayden's back in an attempt to calm him. Jayden merely pulled the guy and slammed him again. The guy's head hit the wall.

Maxwell got between them. The man lifted his arms up.

'What's the racket—' began Kai, entering from the bedroom, buttoning his shirt. He stopped short. 'Ron.' His face betrayed contempt.

'Ron? That's Ron?' Maxwell seethed at the guy, '*You're* Ron?'

'Lovers, please.' Kai walked straight to Ron, his posture authoritative, and asserted, 'I don't know how you found me or what you want, but I don't care. You need to leave. If I ever see you again, I'll get a restraining order.'

Maxwell observed Kai – he was uncertain if this was difficult for him but Kai maintained a serene expression.

'Kai, baby, you're the only one for me.'

Maxwell didn't like another man who wasn't part of their trio calling Kai that.

'I've been looking all over for you. You never showed—'

'Four years!' Kai raised his voice. 'You would have found me before. Needing a fix of emotional supply? I won't ever again be that for you, Ron.'

Ron reached towards Kai. Jayden twitched but Maxwell put a hand out to stop him. Kai needed to be the one to stop Ron, for the sake of Jayden knowing Kai wasn't choosing Ron over them. Maxwell knew the heaviness that this weighed on both Jayden and Kai, more than it did on him. Maxwell trusted Kai and wanted Jayden to see why.

As soon as Ron's hand reached close enough to Kai's face, Kai slapped it away.

'Four years ago when I left to meet with you, I was hit by a car.' Ron's eyes widened. Kai continued. 'I was in a coma for *three years*.'

Kai stepped back and reached his hands out behind him towards his lovers. Maxwell came to stand on one side, Jayden on the other, and Kai interlaced their hands. His grip was firm but relaxed, assertive and confident – more like he was conveying reassurance rather than needing support.

'You see these two men? They are my fiancés. I have dedicated myself to them, and only them.'

'If you're sharing, I can share too. Kai, I need—'

'No, Ron.' Kai remained calm but his tone was calculatedly raised.

Maxwell grew nervous. Ron's tone was manipulative, convincing. His heart thudded; Jayden tensed.

Kai squeezed both their hands and it reassured them – both relaxed immediately.

'I don't want you in my life, Ron.'

'You're just saying that. Let me remind you—'

'I don't need you.'

* * *

Kai thought this would be more difficult, but the words came easily, for the feelings he once had for Ron were completely gone. He sized Ron up and down, wondering why he ever felt weak around him before, why he had been drawn to him, now finding him unappealing. And yet, he knew why.

'That accident was a wake-up call. It jolted me, and I am never breaking my promise to myself again, my promise to Jayden, my promise to Maxwell.'

'But you always come back to me. Because it's *me* you want. I can be for you what these men can't.'

Kai let out a condescending chuckle before sobering again. 'Not anymore – if ever that was true. But it wasn't, I just fell for your lies. Not anymore.'

Kai pointed at the open door. 'Leave. Before I call the cops on you.'

Ron reached pleadingly towards Kai. 'Kai, I know you need me.'

Kai laughed, relieved at how wrong Ron was.

'I once thought I did. I once couldn't get you out of my head, no matter how toxic you were for me and *to* me.' Kai let go of Maxwell's hand and pulled out his phone. 'I feel nothing for you, Ron.' It was true – no anger or contempt, no unhealthy longing that loomed like an addiction, not even pity. Nothing.

Kai began to dial. It took Ron a beat to realise Kai wasn't bluffing before he scurried to the door, tripping on himself. 'All right, I'm going.'

Kai shut the door and locked it before Ron could say anything more. He waited until Ron's footsteps receded.

Kai turned to his lovers. 'I mean it, I feel nothing. The accident woke me up. It brought the three of us together, despite the anguish it caused. All I feel, is for the two of you. Anything I thought I felt for Ron got smashed away when that windshield hit my head.'

Maxwell winced visibly, turning his face away.

Kai cupped his cheek. 'I'm sorry. I could have phrased that more gently, but it's true.' Kai turned Maxwell's face to look at him. 'I told you you saved me from that mistake. It's true.' He pressed a soft kiss to Maxwell's lips. Maxwell nodded.

Jayden hesitated, shuffling a foot. 'You didn't – don't – feel anything at all for Ron anymore?'

Kai smiled at Jayden. 'Nothing. My heart swells with love for you, baby. For both of you.' Kai closed his eyes, taking a deep breath. He then looked deep into his lovers' eyes, his smile wide. 'I'm free.'

Maxwell wrapped his strong arms around Kai as Jayden lunged to claim his lips for a fiery and relieved kiss.

When he pulled away, Kai added, 'I have never been more ready to marry you than now.' Kai interlaced his fingers with both Jayden and Maxwell. 'I am ready to be your husband.'

'I am ready to be your husband,' the other two echoed.

Kai was overjoyed. His relief made his eyes water and he pulled the men he loved close, holding them both tightly. 'I promise to dedicate the rest of my life to you both, and the two of you only.'

'There is no one else for me either,' voiced Maxwell. 'It was strange at first, our circumstances, but I love you, and I'll be the best husband I can be to both of you, to meet your needs.'

'And to always be honest,' completed Jayden. 'To devote my passion and my trust to the two of you with all of my being.'

* * *

The three men pulled away from each other, hands clasped tightly as they reiterated their trinity of affection.

'Undying love,' said Jayden.

'Everlasting healing,' said Kai.

'Freeing forgiveness,' said Maxwell.

Maxwell and Kai took Jayden's ring and together slipped it on his finger. Maxwell and Jayden did the same for Kai. And then, Kai and Jayden slid Maxwell's ring on his finger.

It was done, they were married. With tears welling in their eyes, the three husbands drew close and pressed a kiss to each other's lips, the three of them locked in their triangle of love, their trinity of affection.

<u>THANK YOU SO MUCH FOR READING</u>

If you enjoyed this story,
please consider taking a few moments
to write a review on Amazon or Goodreads.
It would mean so much.

Thank you.

<u>Also By</u>

Also Written by Eidahs

Sanguine Sincerity
Primal Passion
(https://binkyproductions.com/Tenebrarum)

The Thief and His Hunter Book 1
The Thief and His Hunter Book 2
(https://binkyproductions.com/TheThiefandHisHunter)

Like Father, Not Like Sons
Legacy Takedown
Of Sullied Dreams and Beaten Hearts
Butchery At the Debauchery
Serendipitous Tribulation
Turbulent Justice
A Romance to Freedom and Pride
(https://binkyproductions.com/shortstories)

You will find more books
published by Binky Ink at:
https://binkyproductions.com/books

About the Author

Eidahs is a pseudonym for all mature written works, from thrillers to erotic romance. Eidahs in pronunciation sounds elven in nature, which is why she chose it, to tap into her love of fantasy, a genre that couples well with super-natural and preternatural, dark fantasy, and romance.

Eidahs is also the nickname 'Shadie' backwards, representing the shadow self, innermost desires, and a spectrum of emotions, most notably, passion, sorrow, rage, and delight, which Eidahs loves to incorporate in her writing. Enticing readers and evoking the characters' emotions when she writes has guided her inspiration to spell many short stories on Medium and a series of books under this pen name.

Connect with Binky Ink:

WordPress Website & Blog
    https://binkyproductions.com/binkyinkwriting
Medium – Main Profile
    https://medium.com/@BinkyInkWriting
X (Twitter) https://twitter.com/binkyinkwriting
Inkitt: https://inkitt.com/eidahs

www.ingramcontent.com/pod-product-compliance
Lightning Source LLC
Chambersburg PA
CBHW071201300726
48975CB00004B/1241